Those eyes... they weren't...

They weren't like... ever seen....

And then she blinked, and Michael's eyes were once again the eyes into which she had looked all day, alight with passion, gentled by regret. "Good night, Aggie," he said. And he left her.

Aggie stood at the window long after he had disappeared into the shadows, wondering if he was out there somewhere, watching her, too. She stood until the moon came up and the mist began to dance on the lake.

Then, shivering, she turned and locked the door.

Rebecca Flanders has written over seventy books under a variety of pseudonyms. She lives in the mountains of north Georgia with a collie, a golden retriever and three cats. In her spare time she enjoys painting, hiking, dog training and catching up on the latest bestsellers.

REBECCA FLANDERS

SECRET OF
THE WOLF

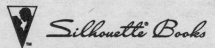

Published by Silhouette Books
America's Publisher of Contemporary Romance

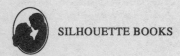

SILHOUETTE BOOKS

ISBN 0-373-51204-X

SECRET OF THE WOLF

Visit Silhouette at www.eHarlequin.com

Printed in U.S.A.

CHAPTER ONE

It was on nights like this, Grandma Maudie used to say, that ghosts and ghoulies stalked the earth, and beasts took on human form to walk amongst us. Grandma Maudie had had quite an imagination, which was where, the family maintained, Agatha McDonald, renowned columnist for the Seattle *Review,* got her talent.

Aggie herself wasn't sure about that, but she did wish Grandma Maudie had been a little more discriminating about the stories she told impressionable young children. On a night like tonight, with the fog rolling in like a tidal wave and the darkness thick enough to cut, the last thing she needed to have creeping about the corners of her mind were imaginary ghosts and ghoulies.

Aggie hated to drive at night. The only reason she had chosen to buy a house so far out of town was that she had been confident she wouldn't have to commute since she worked from home. Now here she was, driving these lonely back roads after dark three days out of five. On nights like this, she virtually *longed* for that Seattle high rise overlooking the Sound.

The fog was so thick, it swallowed her headlights whole, and returned the ghostly remainder of the light to her in a sickly wavering smoke screen. Aggie constantly leaned forward to wipe her windshield, only to discover that the opacity was on the outside and beyond her reach. The road was narrow and winding, and she crept along at a cowardly twenty-five miles per hour, crouching over the steering wheel as though proximity to the windshield would improve her vision. She turned up the radio for company, but the whiny, tinny cowboy tune only served to emphasize the loneliness of the road, as though she, falsely secure inside her car, were the last living being on earth.

"Thank you, Grandma Maudie," she muttered, pushing the maudlin thought aside with a shake. She even tried to sing along with the cowboy tune for a while, but soon found herself clutching the steering wheel again, squinting earnestly at the windshield.

It was dark, the kind of dark that seemed to be more than a simple absence of light. There were no streetlights, no starlight, no radiant light from nearby houses. Just dark. It was a hungry dark, a greedy dark, an empty dark.

And suddenly, the dark wasn't empty anymore.

Two phosphorescent eyes appeared before her, seeming to be suspended in midair in the fog. She was so horrified, so completely caught off guard by what she saw that for one crucial moment, she couldn't believe her eyes—she thought Grandma Maudie's gruesome tales had started to unravel before her, and she simply couldn't react. By the time she did react, it was too late.

She slammed on the brakes only a split second before she felt something thud against her front fender and heard an animal's startled yelp of pain. Aggie screamed as the wheels started to skid on the slick pavement, and she fought wildly for control. The back wheels slid off the road and onto the shoulder, where, after one more terrifying moment, they gained traction and Aggie was able to bring the car to a solid stop.

She rested her head on the steering wheel, the pounding of her heart shaking her whole body, gasping for breath. *Oh God,* she thought over and over again because she didn't have the strength to say it out loud. *Oh, God...*

It was some time before her limbs stopped shaking enough that she could make them do what she commanded them to do. Fumbling for the flashlight that she kept in the glove box for just such emergencies, Aggie got out of the car.

She stepped out into another world.

The car door clicked shut behind her with a muffled, faraway sound, and the shape of the vehicle was lost in the fog. It was as if she had stepped from a time machine, which was now disappearing into the nether regions from whence it had come. The yellow glow of her flashlight beam penetrated a feeble two feet into the fog, and her footsteps made a hollow sound on the shrouded pavement as she moved forward.

"Dog?" she called timidly. "Here, pooch! Where are you?"

She couldn't bear the thought of the poor animal lying in a ditch somewhere, its cries too weak for her to hear. But she dreaded even more the other possibility—that he could no longer cry at all. Of course, she hadn't been going very fast; it was possible she had only struck the dog a glancing blow and he had run off into the woods. *Please,* she prayed silently, *let that be what happened. Don't let it be...*even in her thoughts she had to hesitate over the word. *Dead.*

She moved deeper and deeper into the fog, carefully swinging the flashlight beam back and forth for a clue. Tension gripped the back of her neck and cold wet fingers of fog whispered over her face. She couldn't see anything. She couldn't feel anything. She was completely alone.

And then the beam of her flashlight picked up something on the ground, half in and half out of the ditch. Aggie moved forward quickly, and then stopped. The flashlight jerked convulsively as she focused on what she had found. It was a human hand.

Aggie dropped to her knees beside the body, shaking uncontrollably as she realized what had happened. It wasn't a dog her car had struck.

It was a man.

Aggie was amazed by how instinct took over, and she reacted with a quick and rational calm that would have been remarkable under circumstances far less trying than these. The first thing she did was steady the flashlight for one quick sweep over his body, looking for obvious wounds.

The man was completely naked. While the more competent part of her mind took note of his condition, she could not ignore the broad, strong back and shoulders glistening slightly with mist and sweat. One arm stretched over his head and was crisscrossed with scratches, none of them very deep. He was extremely lean, his ribs clearly visible and his waist spare. His buttocks were tight and muscular, his thighs strong and covered with dark hair. A huge purple bruise was already beginning to swell on the thigh closest to her, presumably where her car had struck him. His legs were long and lean and covered with scrapes and scratches; his feet were filthy.

He had long, brownish hair that fell forward to obscure his face. She pushed it back, searching for a carotid pulse and held her breath until she felt the beat, slow but strong, against her fingers.

"Thank you," she whispered into the mist. "Thank you…"

She dared not move him, even to try to turn him over. She shrugged out of her raincoat and draped it over him, then ran back to her car.

Her older brother, David, had nagged her into purchasing a car phone as soon as she'd started commuting regularly from the suburbs. He worked in the emergency room of one of Seattle's busiest hospitals, and he saw too many illustrations of the kinds of emergencies that could happen on the road. Until now, the only emergency for which Aggie had used the phone was to make dinner reservations when she was stuck in traffic; she thought of it as little more than an expensive toy. But at that moment, she could have kissed David's feet for making her buy it.

She dialed 911 and waited an interminable time for a connection before she realized she had forgotten to push Send. She took several deep breaths and tried not to peer too desperately into the darkness to where she had left the injured man. Her call was answered on the third ring.

"I need an ambulance," she gasped, speaking quickly as though by doing so she could hurry the response. "A man—I hit him with my car…I never saw him, I swear I didn't. He's hurt, I don't know how badly. Hurry, please!"

"Your location, ma'am?"

Aggie told the dispatcher as much as she could about where she was, and he told her that help was on the way. Aggie turned on the hazard flashers of her car, grabbed the flashlight and ran back to where she had left the man, half expecting him to have disappeared into the mist while she was gone, leaving her with nothing more than the memory of a bad nightmare.

But he wasn't gone, and this wasn't a nightmare. He still lay, quiet and unmoving, covered by her coat. He was so still, in fact, that another shaft of panic struck her and she dropped to the ground beside him, searching again for the pulse in his neck. His skin was warm, his pulse was palpable. She released a shaky breath of relief.

"Don't you dare die on me," she muttered. "Just—don't you dare. Hold on, just a little while longer. Help is coming."

The stranger moaned and shifted his head a little.

A stab of anxiety went through Aggie's nerves and she leaned forward quickly, stroking his hair soothingly. Whatever he had been through—and it must have been quite some ordeal to have brought him to this point, naked and bleeding beside a country road—his hair was in wonderful shape. It felt like satin beneath her fingers.

"It's okay," she whispered. "Don't try to move. You're going to be fine."

He opened his eyes, and Aggie jerked back, startled. He winced and closed his eyes again almost immediately because the beam of the flashlight was shining directly in them, but not before Aggie got a glimpse of something—it was too quick to define—but something about his eyes…something strange.

"Mister?" Cautiously, she touched his shoulder, her heart pounding hard.

The only response was another muffled moan and he did not open his eyes again. Aggie sat back anxiously and strained her ears for the sound of an approaching siren. She kept her hand on his shoulder, half convinced, in a foolishly superstitious way, that as long as she was touching him, he wouldn't slip away from her.

And perhaps it worked, because when the ambulance arrived less than ten minutes later with its busy crew of trained paramedics and high-tech equipment, he was still breathing steadily, still flickering in and out of consciousness. The police cars were only moments behind, and they descended on Aggie with endless questions—so many and so demanding that she didn't have time to ask questions of her own. The last she saw of the stranger was when the stretcher upon which he was strapped was being lifted into the ambulance.

She called out, "St. Vincent's?"

"That's right!" the paramedic replied, then he slammed the ambulance doors and ran around to the front.

The ambulance raced off into the night, leaving nothing but an eerie glow of swirling orange lights in its wake.

Aggie hated the emergency room of St. Vincent's Hospital, and she knew it better than possibly any other place in Seattle. Not only was her brother on staff here, but back in the days when she was a cub reporter for the Seattle *Review,* a great many of her stories had started—or ended—there. The atmosphere of subdued chaos, the cheap brown Naugahyde seats, the stale coffee, the smell of disinfectant—none of it had changed. And she still hated it.

She got up and approached the desk. "Any word?"

Colleen, the duty nurse, glanced up from her computer terminal and shook her head. "I'll let you know."

"You told David, didn't you? He knows I'm here?"

Colleen looked at her sympathetically. "Are you sure you won't let me get you a sedative? You've been through a trauma, and—"

"I'm not the patient here! I'm trying to find *out* about a patient here and I don't seem to be able to do even that. What is it with you people? I swear to—"

"So, McDonald. What's the word?"

Colleen shot a relieved look over Aggie's shoulder to Russ Lane, the police officer assigned to the case. Suddenly, Aggie felt embarrassed at having taken out her anxiety on Colleen. She muttered, "Nothing. No word." Then, to Colleen, "I'm sorry I yelled at you."

Colleen shrugged amiably. "I've heard worse. Listen, all I can tell you is he's out of X ray and they didn't send him down to surgery. That's usually a good sign."

The phone rang and Colleen turned to answer it.

Aggie swallowed hard. "Or not."

Russ touched her shoulder. "Here. I brought you some coffee."

Aggie looked at the white foam cup and grimaced. "No thanks. Any more of that goop and I *will* be climbing the walls."

Russ sipped from the cup blandly. "It's not that bad."

The big double doors swung open and Russ and Aggie moved quickly out of the way of another incoming stretcher as the emergency team rushed to meet it.

Russ gestured her back toward the alcove with its

Naugahyde chairs and two-year-old magazines. "Busy tonight," he observed.

All the chairs were taken—mostly by relatives and friends of patients, but some by the actual injured—and people were leaning against walls and sitting on the floor. A baby cried incessantly while its mother shifted it from arm to arm and made shushing noises. A group of teenagers played a subdued game of cards on the floor, looking up anxiously whenever an examining-room door opened. A man paced tensely. A young woman cradled her arm against her chest. The sounds from the adjacent examining rooms were not pleasant.

"Full moon," Aggie said, repressing a shudder. "David says it always gets crazy."

"He's got that right. For us, too. All things considered, though, I'd rather be in here waiting to complete my report than out on the streets tonight."

"Yeah," agreed Aggie absently. "Russ, how do you think he ended up like that—out in the middle of nowhere, miles from any house, with no clothes on?"

Russ looked at her soberly. "The truth?"

Aggie hesitated, swallowing a lump of uneasiness in her throat, and nodded.

"Beats the hell out of me," Russ said.

Aggie's shoulders sagged.

He sipped his coffee. "He looks a little old for a school hazing prank—mid-thirties, wouldn't you say? But there are all kinds of weird cults and clubs out there. Maybe it was some kind of initiation. Maybe it was a joke that got out of hand. He could have been the victim of a crime. Whatever it was, we're not going to know until he tells us."

Aggie ran her hand through her short auburn hair,

pushing it away from her face, then nervously combing the bangs forward again. ''There was a dog,'' she
said distractedly.

''What?''

''He had a dog. At least I think he did. I thought it
was the dog I'd hit, but when I looked for it, it was
gone.''

Russ frowned. ''You didn't put that in your statement.''

''Is it important?''

''No, I guess not. But you should have said so.''

''I forgot. I thought I imagined it. I probably did.''

''Probably so,'' Russ agreed with an alacrity that
could have only been inspired by the prospect of the
paperwork involved in amending Aggie's statement.

''Still, I hate to think there's some poor dog wandering around out there, alone and scared.''

''We could notify the SPCA if you like,'' Russ suggested helpfully. ''They could keep an eye out.''

Aggie smiled at him. Russ was a nice man, a rare
find these days. Aggie wished she could be attracted
to him. They had been out a couple of times, but nothing had ever clicked. He just wasn't her type. She was
beginning to suspect, after thirty-four years of looking,
that no one was her type.

That had never bothered her, until recently.

''Thanks, Russ,'' she said. ''But I guess we'd better
wait and ask the patient if he *had* a dog, huh?''

''Wouldn't hurt.''

Aggie paced a few steps away from him, hugging
her arms. ''What is *taking* so long?''

Russ had no answer.

A chill seized her and Aggie stopped pacing, bow-ing her head. "Oh, Russ," she said quietly. "What if he dies?"

"He's not going to die."

Aggie whirled at the sound of her brother's voice.

"At least not any time soon," David McDonald clarified as he moved toward them at an easy pace. "I'd give him—oh, another forty or fifty years. Providing, of course, he stays out of the way of oncoming vehicles, particularly those driven by my sister in her manic phase."

David's sense of humor had never been his strongest point.

"Do you mean he's okay?" Aggie demanded breathlessly. "He's not hurt?"

"He has a mild concussion and some scrapes and bruises. He could stand to gain a few pounds, and he's a little dehydrated. But no broken bones or other major damage."

David tried to shine a penlight in Aggie's eyes, but she jerked her head away. "Stop that. I told you, I wasn't hurt."

"Is it okay if I talk to him? I need to finish up my report," Russ explained.

"Go ahead." David caught Aggie's wrist and placed his thumb over her pulse. "It won't do you much good, though."

Aggie pulled her wrist away impatiently, insisting she wasn't his patient.

"What do you mean?" Russ asked.

"He's suffering from a form of amnesia. He can't remember anything before the accident." He paused for effect. "Not even his name."

Aggie stared at her brother. Russ groaned out loud as the hours he had allotted to this case tripled.

"You've had a shock, Aggie. I'm going to give you something to help you sleep tonight," David told his sister.

"Your assistant pill-pusher already tried that," Aggie responded immediately. "David, are you kidding? Genuine amnesia? He really can't remember his name?"

"I hardly ever kid about a diagnosis. Temporary amnesia isn't all that uncommon with a head injury like his. I'm not alarmed."

He reached into the pocket of his lab coat and pulled out a small brown envelope. "He was wearing this when he came in," he told Russ. As he spoke, he opened the envelope and spilled the contents into the palm of his hand. "It might help."

David held up a gold medallion on a chain. Russ took it from him, and Aggie pushed close to see.

It was an odd piece of jewelry. It was hexagonal and heavily bordered, which suggested a custom-made piece. On one side was a circle with the left half shaded, like a shadowed moon. Aggie frowned a little as she studied it.

"That looks familiar, doesn't it?" she murmured.

"No." Russ turned the medallion over. On that side was the inscription: To Michael the First, From All of Us.

"Michael," Aggie said out loud. "So that's his name."

"Maybe," Russ agreed noncommittally.

He returned the medallion to David, who replaced it in its envelope.

"What do you mean?" Aggie said. "Maybe?"

"I mean he could have stolen it. Did you show that to him?" Russ asked, indicating the medallion.

David nodded. "Nothing."

"Do you think he's faking?"

Aggie interrupted, "Now wait a minute—"

"Hard to tell," David conceded. "I've called in a psychiatric consultant."

"What are you talking about?" Aggie demanded. "The poor man is lying in a strange hospital, hurt, confused—"

"With an awful lot of explaining to do," Russ added. "And a very convenient loss of memory. Come on, McDonald, he was out there running from something. It might well have been the law."

"Naked?" Her tone was dry.

Russ shrugged. "Maybe he's a psycho." Then he sighed. "I guess I'd better go talk to him, anyway. Then we'll have to run him through the computer and see if there's anything on file."

"He's not a psycho," Aggie muttered as Russ left. "He's not a criminal, either."

"Oh, yeah? How do you know?"

Of course, Aggie did not know. She wasn't usually given to sentimentality, and she made a living out of commenting on the ironies of life, but she really did not want to believe that she had been through all of this merely to save the life of someone who was crim-inally insane. So she said defensively, "Well, Michael is the name of an archangel, isn't it?"

"This guy is going to need more than one archangel to get him back together again."

"What are you saying?"

David hesitated, then shook his head. "Nothing. He may have complete recall in the morning. It's just that the system really isn't designed to cope with cases like this, and I see too many of them. In a week, this otherwise bright, capable guy will be out on the street sleeping in doorways and picking through restaurant Dumpsters for his dinner. All because no one has the time—or the money—to try to figure out what's really wrong with him.''

Aggie had no answer for that. She knew the story, too, and David was right. It was far too common.

She glanced down the corridor toward the examining cubicles where he lay. She said, a little uncertainly, "David...did you notice anything unusual about him?''

Something flickered across David's expression. "Like what?''

"Well...'' She hesitated, not exactly sure she, herself, knew what she meant. "Like his eyes. His pupils, actually. Anything odd about them?''

The doctor persona was back. "Equal and reactive. Why?''

Another question she couldn't answer. "Nothing. I must have imagined it.'' But she sensed a slight hesitance on David's part, and she knew her brother too well to let it pass. "What?'' she asked.

"Nothing.'' He started walking toward the desk to pick up his next case. "Medical stuff.''

Aggie followed closely. "Come on. Like what?''

"Nothing. It's just that when you asked if there was something unusual, I wondered how you knew.''

Aggie's patience was at the limit. She caught his arm. "What *are* you talking about?''

He stopped and turned to her. "X rays,'' he explained. The only betrayal of his thoughts was the very faintest edge of a scowl between his eyebrows. "We took several plates—hip, knee, humerus and ulna, just to be on the safe side.''

"And?"

"And in every one of the plates, his joints showed the same—not deformity, really, but peculiarity. They weren't fully seated, if you can picture what I'm saying. Almost the same manifestation you'd see in people who are double-jointed, but not really. As though the bones had been dislocated and reset repeatedly."

"Like Houdini," Aggie murmured.

Now it was David's turn to stare. "What?"

"Houdini," Aggie explained. "He could dislocate his joints at will. That's how he performed his strait-jacket escapes."

David looked skeptical. "Maybe."

"Doctor." Colleen lifted a hand for his attention.

"Aggie, I don't want you driving home tonight. You can stay at my place," David said, moving toward the desk.

Aggie was none too anxious to get back behind the wheel of a car, and she didn't argue. "I need to see him," Aggie said.

David took a chart file from Colleen, but paused to glance at Aggie. Sympathy and understanding were in his eyes. "He's fine," he said. "Really."

Then he nodded toward the corridor. "Examining room three. They'll be moving him upstairs soon, but you've got a few minutes."

"Thanks," Aggie said, and hurried down the corridor.

CHAPTER TWO

Russ was coming out of the room when Aggie reached it. He paused to lift his eyebrows and roll his eyes in an exaggerated gesture of helplessness and frustration. Aggie gave him a brief, understanding smile and promptly forgot about Russ the minute she moved past him into the room.

The man was lying on the high adjustable bed with his shoulders propped up, a thin hospital pillow cushioning his head. A sheet covered him from the waist down, his torso was bare. His hair was chestnut-colored, with a striking platinum streak about an inch wide that formed a widow's peak and feathered toward his shoulders on either side. Though his hair was tangled over his neck and collarbone now, Aggie remembered the luxuriant feel of it beneath her fingers.

He had a broad, aristocratic forehead and a sharp nose. His cheekbones were high, and his lips distinctively shaped, as though sculpted by an artistic hand. There was something vaguely exotic about his face, almost patrician yet at the same time savage, elemental. He could have been a street fighter or a poet, a prince or an assassin. What he could never be was ordinary.

There was a scrape on his right cheekbone and a white gauze patch on his forehead, around the edges of which a reddish-purple bruise was visible. His eyes were closed, and Aggie started to back away. She would not describe herself as particularly cowardly, but this was not an interview she was looking forward to. She had satisfied herself that he was all right—or at least not dependent on life-support equipment—and that was really the reason she had needed to see him for herself. After all, what *did* you say to someone you had almost killed? Perhaps the best thing she could do for him now would be to let him sleep.

She reached behind her for the handle of the door, and his eyes opened. There it was again, for the briefest moment, something about his eyes, his pupils...something that wasn't quite right, something shocking, even unnatural...and then it was gone. He focused his eyes on her with a little frown of exertion, and as hard as she looked, the only unusual thing she noticed about his eyes was their color. They were the most spectacular shade of sapphire blue she had ever seen.

"Hello," he said a little thickly.

Aggie had no choice. She forced a smile and moved closer to his bed. "Hi."

He cleared his throat, studying her intently from his position on the bed. "I'm sorry, I have a ferocious headache, and they might have given me something... Do I know you?"

"No," she assured him awkwardly. "That is, not really."

His eyes moved over her face, searching and scrutinizing, making her want to squirm. "But I do," he insisted slowly. "I know you. I've seen you before..."

"From the accident," Aggie blurted out. "I was the one who—who hit you. I'm so sorry, I swear I never saw you, I never expected anyone to be out there, and I wasn't going fast, I'm a very good driver really, I just never..."

She trailed off as his slow, wide smile made gentle mockery of her babble. He had a wonderful smile. The stuff of royalty and movie stars.

"Had anything like this happen to me before," she finished lamely. Then she added, "Anyway, David—that's my brother, your doctor, Dr. McDonald—says you're going to be okay." Then she couldn't help herself. "What *were* you doing out there, anyway?"

"That would appear to be the question of the moment, wouldn't it?" His eyes moved over her again, the remnants of the gentle smile lingering. "As David, your brother, my doctor, might have told you, I seem to be experiencing a slight problem with recall. I understand my name is Michael, however. I'm sorry I can't supply a last name. Do you have one?"

He was delightful. His voice was a smooth baritone, the rhythm of his speech mesmerizing. Aggie was more or less enchanted, and had a moment's difficulty focusing on his question. "A last name?"

"Or a first one."

"It's Aggie." She took a step closer to the bed; she didn't know why. "Aggie McDonald."

He smiled. "I'm pleased to meet you, Aggie."

"That's gracious of you—under the circumstances."

He started to laugh, then winced and brought a hand to his bandaged head. "Yes, I suppose it is. But don't make me laugh again."

"I should go," she said quickly. She was a little ashamed of how suddenly eager she was to get away from him, but she couldn't help it. It was more than just the awkwardness of confronting the man she had hit with her car. A great deal more.

Michael surprised her, and that made her uneasy.

He was composed, articulate, disarming. There wa⸱ an elemental magnetism about him that was more than a little dangerous. He was not the kind of man one would normally expect to find running around the dark deserted countryside naked. And Aggie had absolutely no business being as intrigued by him as she was.

"No, don't go," he said. And those soft blue eyes held her. "That is," he added politely, "unless you have to."

Aggie hesitated. "I shouldn't tire you."

But she didn't leave. Not immediately.

Then she added, "David said not to worry about the amnesia. It's usually only temporary."

"I'm not worried." He grimaced a little and touched his temple. "Although I may start to when my head stops hurting."

Aggie bit her lip. "I really am awfully sorry."

He looked up at her, and his expression softened. "You smell like pear glacé," he said.

That startled a laugh out of her, and her hands flew immediately to her hair, which she had washed in a new shampoo called Pear Blossom. But that had been two days ago, and she was standing at least five feet away from him. "How could you possibly know that?" she demanded.

He shrugged and grinned disarmingly. "I guess I must have a nose for beautiful things."

Aggie laughed again. "Well, I think your memory loss can't be too severe if you can remember a dessert as elegant as pear glacé. And you must be a lot stronger than you pretend if you're able to come up with lines like that."

"Drat," he said, sinking back against the pillow. "Foiled again."

They spent a moment smiling at each other, and then the door swung open, admitting an orderly pushing a gurney.

"I think this is for you," Aggie said, edging out of the way. "I'll get going now."

"Thank you for coming," he said.

She paused. "Is there anything I can get for you?"

He fingered the thin sheet that covered his nakedness and glanced at her with a wry expression. "Pajamas?"

Aggie grinned. "I'll see what I can do."

She went out into the corridor feeling much better about the entire episode than she had any right to feel, and couldn't help noting the irony in the fact that it had been the patient who had cheered up the visitor, rather than the other way around.

David was standing at the desk, scowling at the receiver he had just slammed into the cradle.

In a much lighter tone than the one with which she had last addressed him, Aggie said, "Problems?"

David started scribbling on a chart in his large, illegible doctor script. "Damn lab," he said. "They screwed up my blood work *again*." He tore off a slip of paper and thrust it at Colleen. "Get them to draw another sample. And I want it stat, I'm tired of being Mr. Nice Guy. And there'd better not be any charge to the patient for this one, I'm checking."

"The patient is indigent," Colleen reminded him, taking the slip.

"All the more reason!"

Aggie said, "This probably isn't a good time, but I wanted to talk to you about Michael. The amnesia patient," she reminded him, just in case.

"As a matter of fact, that's who this is about," David told her, still sounding irritated. "All I wanted was routine blood work and they did something to the sample—damaged it, mislabeled it, who knows? Now they're telling me it's not even human, can you believe that? What a bunch of idiots."

Aggie couldn't explain the chill that went through her. She had a quick vision of those eyes…but again, it was gone before she could pin down the source of her uneasiness.

David said, "I'm sorry. You wanted to ask me something?"

Aggie brought her attention back to him with difficulty. "Oh," she said. Whatever it had been was completely gone now. "No. That's okay. It was nothing. Listen, do you think it would be okay if I came back to see him tomorrow?"

"Sure. He'll be here. You've got your key, right?"

She had already turned toward the door, now she looked back in some confusion. "What?"

"You're staying at my place, right?"

"Oh, yes. Right. Easier than driving home." She patted her leather shoulder bag. "Key's right here. I'll see you later."

"I doubt it," David called after her. "I'm on duty till 2:00 a.m."

But Aggie barely heard him. She pushed open the swinging doors and stepped out into the foggy night, deep in thought.

The mist on his face. The beat of his heart. The smell of blood. Running, running. The sound of his breathing, wind rushing past his ears and something behind him, closer now, gaining every minute. Running, fast, fast…

Michael awoke with a start, his heart roaring in his ears, blood on his hands, the taste of blood in his mouth. Pain racketed through his head and exploded in blue and white waves as he sat up, fumbling to orient himself. But when his vision cleared and he spread out his hands in the dim nighttime hospital light, he could see that they were clean. Trembling, but clean. No blood. The nightmare had been so vivid, it surprised him.

He lay back against the sweat-soaked pillow and tried to breathe deeply. A breath of air from the cooling system struck him and he shivered. After a time, the racing of his heart subsided and his breathing slowed to normal, but he couldn't get the taste of the dream out of his mouth.

He lay there listening to the soft slippery sound of the nurse's crepe-soled shoes on the tile floor far down the corridor; the heavy breathing of the man in the room next to him; a low moan muffled by several walls and a flight of stairs; the murmur of voices; the distant hum of the machinery that made this place work. In the deep hours past midnight in a hospital, even silence had its sounds.

The clatter and hiss from the kitchen three stories down; the squeak of a gurney's wheels on its way to the basement morgue; the sound of highway traffic even farther away… He concentrated on these sounds, trying to erase the memory of the nightmare. And the smells. Alcohol and disinfectant. Laundry soap, penicillin, sickness, the stale, flat smell of death…the faint wisp of perfume. He concentrated. Eternity, not fresh, but applied several days ago and now clinging to a garment that was hanging in a closet several rooms away… Eternity. It made his nose tickle.

He smiled in the darkness, beginning to relax. He could remember a perfume but not his own name. Was that a good sign? It was probably better, he decided, than remembering nothing at all.

The remnants of the nasty dream were beginning to fade because thinking about perfume reminded him of the scent of pears and the lovely red-haired woman who wore it. Aggie McDonald. Green eyes that sparkled like sun on the water when she smiled, skin the color of rich cream, thick cinnamon-colored hair that she wore cropped short in an oddly endearing style. Aggie McDonald and pear glacé, each of them delectably sensuous in its own way, tart and sweet and sinfully self-indulgent. Just thinking about her made him feel better. He hoped he would see her again.

But even that small reminder of the future—wondering whether or not he would see Aggie again—stirred up an anxiety within him, and he couldn't stay in bed any longer. He stood up carefully, subduing the throbbing in his head by sheer force of will, and walked to the window. The hospital gown with which they had provided him was drafty and uncomfortable and looked ridiculous but it was better than being naked.

He moved aside the metal blinds a fraction and stared out over the parking lot, frowning. What *had* he been doing in the middle of the deserted countryside, running through the night with no clothes on? Was there any acceptable reason for such an event? And why couldn't he remember? Was it, as the doctor had suggested, a not-uncommon result of his head injury, or was there something more? Was it possibly because he didn't want to remember?

And what would become of him if he *never* remembered?

Or, perhaps even worse—what if he did remember and couldn't live with the answer? After all, he had been running from something.

He pushed back the blinds farther and turned his head toward the sky, looking for the moon. He couldn't see it, and after a moment, he let the blinds fall back into place and turned away from the window.

But he did not go back to bed. He sat in the room's single chair to await the dawn, not bothering to turn on the light. He knew he would not sleep again tonight. He didn't know what horrors lurked in his past nor what new torments tomorrow might bring, but he did know what awaited him in sleep. And the dreams were one thing he was not willing to face.

Single in Seattle
by Aggie McDonald

All Shook Up

Every once in a while, my Grandma Maudie used to say, it's good for a person to get a little shaken up. The pipes that burst and rain three thousand gallons of city water into your newly decorated home (who do you call to clean it up, anyway?); the burglar who drops in to relieve you of everything you own and makes six hundred dollars' worth of overseas calls on your telephone before stealing that, as well; the old boyfriend who spots you at the supermarket when you're ten pounds overweight and having the worst hair day of your life; the cat who runs away; the dog who won't run away; the mysterious stranger who steps out of the night and into the path of your on-coming car. These are the little tragedies and misfor-tunes of life, the unexpected challenges, the unwel-come surprises.

They're never much fun, and despite what Grandma Maudie claims, I've never known them to do much toward building character. But these potholes and pit-falls on the great highway of life do have one inter-esting side effect: They shake you up. They make you do a double take, step back and look again at the com-fortable rut your life was in. And chances are, you won't look at it in the same way again.

You remember Grandma Maudie. She's the one who is also responsible for such gems as, "If you swallow a watermelon seed, it'll grow inside your stomach until you swell up and burst" and "How do you ever expect to catch a husband if you can't make biscuits?" God rest her. But now and then, the dear old soul did have something to say worth listening to. Like "If it's not picked ripe, it's not worth eating" and "The Republicans can't stay in power forever." And "It does a person good to get shook up every once in a while."

My pipes didn't burst; I wasn't burgled; I gave up on cats three years ago; and I wasn't caught looking my worst by an old boyfriend—not this week, anyway. I was, however, involved in what the police euphe-mistically refer to as a "pedestrian-vehicular acci-dent." I hit a man with my car. And let me tell you, nothing looks quite the same after that.

Aggie scrolled through the article on her computer screen, rereading it, and she thought, *This is good. This is damn good.*

That was the first time she had been able to say that

about anything she had written in a long time—longer than she liked to think about.

"Single in Seattle" was one of the *Review's* most popular features, and Aggie knew that it would take more than a few bad columns to turn her readers away. But she was not nearly as forgiving of herself as was the reading public, and lately she couldn't help noticing that her columns had gotten a little stale.

That, perhaps, was putting it gently. *Moldy* might be more accurate. Twice in the past month alone, she had failed to produce so much as a single misspelled word, forcing her editor to rerun some of her old columns. That was embarrassing, not because she'd failed to meet a deadline—it happened to every columnist sooner or later—but because the old columns were so much better than the ones she was writing now. Most writers improved with time. She was deteriorating.

She was even beginning to think about giving it up.

The subject matter—the trials, tribulations, triumphs and pithy observations of a single woman in the big city—no longer inspired her as it once had. She'd started to feel more like a syndicated cartoon character than a commentator on the nineties. What was so fascinating about laundry-room dating, anyway? The Clarence Thomas hearings were old news and you could only get so much mileage, so to speak, out of carpooling laws that discriminate against singles. Being single in the nineties just wasn't interesting anymore. She was running out of material.

But last night, far too keyed up to sleep, she had instinctively turned to the only remedy that had never failed her in any situation before—writing out her feelings. She'd closed the door to David's apartment-size study and sat down at his computer and written until the city lights had blinked out one by one and dawn had turned the sky from gray to pink to a welcome, surprising, partly cloudy sapphire blue.

Like the color of his eyes.

Where did he come from? No one knows. Where will he go? He's not sure. He has a first name, but no last. He has no friends, no family—or if he does, he hasn't the first idea where to find them. He doesn't own a thing in this world, not even his own identity.

Once he might have been an engineer, a film-maker, an artist, a doctor. He might have built the bridge you cross every day to get to work or de-signed the replacement heart valve that saved your father's life or written the music that brings a tear to your eye every time you hear it. Today, he's nameless, penniless, homeless. Nobody. And it happened in the blink of an eye.

It could be you. It could be me.

It shook me up.

Thanks, Granda Maudie. You did it again.

Good stuff.

With a brisk confidence she hadn't felt in a long time, Aggie faxed the column to her editor, along with a note advising him that she would see him for lunch. She showered and changed into a pair of jeans left over from the last time she had stayed with David, while her house was being painted, and a silk shirt she had found hanging in the guest-room closet that was *not* hers but looked great on her and which she figured its owner deserved to lose for being so careless with her possessions.

She propped a note for David against the saltshaker on the kitchen table, helped herself to a bagel and was on the streets by seven-thirty.

An idea was beginning to form.

CHAPTER THREE

Rumor had it that Seattle was the wettest city in the United States. This was not strictly true. Precipitation actually averaged no more than any East Coast city; it was just that all of Seattle's precipitation came in the form of rain, with no relief from snow or ice. Most of that rain fell in the winter, during which the sun might not be seen for months on end. Seattle had earned its reputation for having the highest per capita population of book readers and film goers by virtue of the short gloomy days and the nights that last up to sixteen hours. No one had ever done a study on what the Seattle night did for romance, but Aggie was not the first to notice that the birthrate soared in August— nine months after the onset of those long, long nights.

But while Seattle might well deserve its reputation for gloom in the winter, spring and fall in the city could be truly spectacular. This bright late-August day was adequate recompense for the nine months of drizzle and fog that had led up to it, and to Aggie it seemed a harbinger of good things.

The magnificent visage of Mount Rainier awaited her as she drove east through the city toward First Hill, where St. Vincent's was located. Until David's student loans were paid last year and he had been able to afford the condo he now owned, he had lived within a block of where he worked, and the commute had been much easier. He and Aggie had moved at approximately the same time, the only difference being

that Aggie's move had represented a change of life-
style, his merely a change of address.

Traffic in Seattle always moved slower when the
sun was shining, and it was after eight o'clock before
she reached the hospital. She went directly to the third
floor and found Vivian Ritcher, head of social services, sipping a cup of coffee at the nurse's desk while
she made notes on a chart. Aggie did not have to guess
whose chart it was.

"Hi," Aggie greeted her. "I don't suppose I could
persuade you to share a vending-machine doughnut
and some stimulating conversation in the lounge,
could I?"

Vivian glanced up with a wry expression. "Well,
speak of the devil," she commented. "As it happens,
I'm very bribable today. And I'll just bet I can guess
the topic of that stimulating conversation you have in
mind."

Vivian gathered up the chart and came out from
behind the horseshoe-shaped desk, coffee cup in hand.

"You wouldn't be wrong," Aggie assured her. She
dug in her purse for change for the vending machine.
"You wouldn't have seventy-five cents, would you?"

Vivian rolled her eyes, shifted her collection of papers and her coffee cup to the other hand, and pro-
ceeded to search her pockets for change.

By the time they reached the lounge, Vivian had
produced three quarters, a crumpled grocery receipt
and a lint-covered piece of hard candy from the pockets of her lab coat. She settled down at one of the
tables while Aggie fed the quarters into the vending
machine and was rewarded with a plastic-wrapped
pastry.

"I was going to interview you, anyway," Vivian said, opening a file folder.

"Good. You can write this off as a business expense." Aggie popped the pastry into the microwave for ten seconds.

"Very funny. What *do* you know about this fellow, anyway? Anything that might help me decide what to do with him?"

The microwave chimed and Aggie opened the door, carefully lifting out the pastry by one corner of its hot, inflated plastic wrapping. "What do you mean, do with him?"

"I'm a bureaucrat, Aggie," Vivian explained patiently. "In my business, everyone has to fit into a predefined compartment or he doesn't exist, haven't you figured that out yet? As for Michael Doe—"

"Is that what they're calling him?" Aggie poured herself a cup of coffee and sat down next to Vivian, dumping the pastry on the table between them.

"Last name unknown. First name, middle initial, none. You've got to fill in all the blanks. As I was saying, he's a hard one to place. He appears to be indigent, but he can't apply for financial assistance without a social security number. We can't trace his social security number without his name and birthday. And that's not even to mention the problems with discharge. The man doesn't have a penny to his name, no idea where his home is, whether or not any family might be looking for him..."

Aggie said, smiling, "You've talked to him?"

Vivian returned a somewhat sheepish grin. "All right, so he's a charmer. And maybe I *am* a little bit more concerned with his case than I would be with the average homeless patient. But you've got to admit, his situation is a little different.''

Aggie slit open the wrapping of the pastry with a plastic knife and cut the roll down the middle. ''He hasn't gotten back *any* of his memory?''

Vivian shook her head, picking up her half of the pastry. ''Nothing important. Dr. Scherer was in with him this morning.''

It was not yet ten o'clock, but already half a day's work had been done on this floor. Morning had an entirely different meaning in a hospital than in the rest of the world.

''I don't know him,'' Aggie said.

''Psychiatric consultant. David ordered an assessment last night.''

Aggie nodded, remembering, and bit into the pastry.

''Anyway, the news is not entirely good for our patient. It's hard to tell in all that gobbledygook psychiatrist scribble, but I think Scherer believes the amnesia is not entirely related to the injury. That there might be some kind of emotional or psychological trauma involved. If that's the case, they'll recommend outpatient treatment, but he can't be admitted. I checked at the desk and the standard discharge on a concussion like his is within twenty-four to forty-eight hours. So, at best, Mr. Doe has one more night of food and shelter before he's turned out onto the street.'' She sighed. ''It's a rotten system, but it's the only one we've got.''

Aggie sipped her coffee, her expression thoughtful. ''Maybe, there's another way,'' she said slowly.

Michael caught the scent of her before she pushed open the door, before he even heard her footsteps on the tile corridor. Sweet, rich. The scent of pears, fainter now than it had been yesterday, overlaid by sugar and cinnamon, coffee and soap. Aggie, with short bouncy hair and a smile full of sun.

Aggie.

He did not know what he had forgotten, but he was glad his memory began with her.

"Hi," she said, pushing open the door a few inches and peeking through the crack before entering the room. "Are you decent?"

"That's a relative term, isn't it?"

She grinned and came in all the way. "All things considered, yes."

She dug into her big, foldover-style purse and produced a flat package enclosed in a folded paper sack. "Some people might have brought flowers," she said, and handed it to him. "I thought these would be more practical."

He smiled as he looked into the sack. Pale blue cotton pajamas, still in their original wrapping. "An excellent choice. Thank you."

"They're my brother's. He has stacks of them in his dresser that people have been giving him for birthdays and Christmases for years. I guess no one bothered to ask him whether he sleeps in pajamas, or not."

"Then thank your brother for me."

"Sorry they're not silk," she commented, sitting down on the chair across from the bed. "Somehow, I picture you in silk—not, of course, that I spend a lot of time picturing you in your pajamas."

She actually blushed a little, and at any other time, Michael would have found the reaction enchanting, but now he barely noticed. Something flickered across the back of his mind...a dark paisley robe, yes, it was silk, cool against his skin; cordovan leather slippers, butter soft, the taste of...

"Bourbon," he murmured out loud.

"What?"

He focused on her again. "I used to drink bourbon," he said.

She looked interested. "Well, that's a start. Has anything else come back to you?"

He shook his head—gingerly, because it still hurt—and gestured with the remote control in his hand. "Before you came in, I was trying to watch the news shows, hoping something would trigger my memory. It all seemed familiar to me, but nothing was specific."

Aggie said, "I checked with the police before I came up. No one's filed a missing person report that fits your description yet—at least not locally. It will take them a few days to cross-reference other areas."

"What about criminal records?"

The way she hesitated made him smile, albeit wryly. "Don't tell me you didn't ask—or that they're not checking."

Aggie lifted her chin in a gesture of instinctive defiance. "Of course they're checking. They'd be crazy not to. And, no. They haven't found anything—yet."

That amused him, and he rested his head on his pillow, smiling, watching her. "So, tell me, Aggie McDonald, what do you think they will find?"

The question did not intimidate her, and she didn't dissemble. Michael liked that.

She returned his gaze thoughtfully and replied, "I don't think they're going to find anything. If you are a criminal, you're far too smart to allow anything about your activities to appear in an FBI file…or maybe just too powerful.''

He lifted an eyebrow. ''An interesting theory. Do you know something I don't?''

''I was a big-city reporter for ten years,'' she informed him. ''I learned a thing or two about types. And your type is…'' She tilted her head a little as she examined him, choosing her words. ''Successful. You're educated, articulate, self-confident—not the qualities of an ordinary street thug.''

''Perhaps I'm a jewel thief,'' he suggested, falling into the game.

''Maybe,'' she agreed easily. ''But I don't really think you operate on that side of the law at all.''

''And why is that?''

''Because a successful criminal—and we've already established you would be successful—wouldn't have allowed himself to get into the situation you were in last night.''

He nodded thoughtfully. ''And a successful jewel thief would have, presumably, been able to at least steal himself a pair of pants.''

She tried not to laugh, but her eyes danced. ''That would be my theory.''

And then she sobered. ''So I think it's more likely you were the victim of a crime of some kind. Or maybe…''

Her eyes dropped.

''Or maybe I'm simply insane,'' he supplied for her with surprising equanimity. He had given the matter considerable thought during the night and it seemed, to him, a reasonable explanation, and one that invoked very little emotion at all. ''Maybe I simply stepped out of the shower yesterday and went for a walk.

Maybe it's common among my kind to run around unclothed in the middle of the night. Maybe it's some kind of rite of passage. Maybe—''

She interrupted curiously, "What do you mean, your kind?''

He was surprised. "What?''

"You said, 'Maybe it's common among my kind,'" she repeated patiently. "What did you mean by that?''

He thought about it for a moment, and there was something…something he didn't want to think about, something he couldn't quite grasp. Something that gave him a chill.

He shook his head, and opened his hands in a gesture of helplessness. "I honestly have no idea,'' he said.

Aggie leaned forward a little in her chair. "Michael, don't you have *any* feelings or impressions about your past? Maybe not definite memories, but hunches or ideas or just plain *feelings.*''

He tried to give her question the consideration it deserved, but the truth was he didn't *want* to think about it. He had impressions, yes. A place he belonged, a cold place with high walls, a place to which he did not want to return. An ice-white moon, wandering in and out of shadowing clouds, chasing him with its relentless light. Running. Blood on his hands, in his hair…

But that was only a nightmare, a dream. There were other impressions, far more fleeting, not nearly as disturbing. The clink of fine crystal. Candlelight, firelight. The smell of leather. The view from a high place, city lights. The strains of an orchestra. A woman's smile. Not a lover. A…mother? People who cared for him. People who *knew* him.

But whenever he tried to grasp one of those impressions, they turned amorphous, drifting through the sieve of his mind like ashes, and almost before he could articulate the thought, he could no longer recall whether he had in fact remembered anything at all. There were good things in his past, he felt sure of that. But he also believed that they were gone forever, and that they had been gone before his memory loss began. He was very much afraid, in fact, that the thing that had taken them from him was the very thing he was afraid to remember.

He tried to smile but the effort strained at his lips and was not very convincing. "There are moments," he admitted, "when I almost remember something, but it's never clear and never lasts long enough for me to capture. I think…" He frowned, concentrating, trying to remember for no more reason than he wanted to please her. "I think I worked in an office once. In a tall building."

Aggie beamed at him. "There, you see, that's a start. That's a terrific start!"

And her excitement faded into concern as she added, "I really can't imagine what it must be like not to remember anything about your past. Not to have anyone to turn to or anywhere to go, not to even know your own name."

"It's…unsettling," he admitted slowly. "To have no anchor, nothing to look back on, nothing to look forward to…or dread. No guilt, no responsibility, no connections. It's a little terrifying." And he smiled reflectively. "And very liberating."

He looked into her eyes, and he could tell that she seemed to understand. She was a remarkable woman. And she had beautiful eyes.

He said, "It's good of you to take such an interest."

She lifted her shoulders in a subtly self-mocking gesture of dismissal. "You know that old Chinese saying that once you save a life, you're responsible for it? I'm not sure what they say regarding someone who almost kills another person, but it's got to be similar."

She seemed nervous, suddenly, and he wanted her to relax. "So, I owe my good fortune to the Chinese, do I?"

"I'm not exactly sure I'd call it good fortune."

And then she shielded those pretty green eyes with her lashes as she focused on one jean-clad knee, brushing at an imaginary smudge. "Actually, my motives aren't entirely unselfish," she admitted.

She looked up at him, uncertainty and determination battling each other in her eyes. "Look," she said. "I'd like to help you. But I need your cooperation—and your permission—first."

He did not point out that he was hardly in a position to refuse her anything. "Sounds interesting," he said. "Go on."

Aggie leaned forward, her arms on her knees, her expression intent and alive with an inner excitement. "Okay," she said with a breath. "Here's my plan."

Aggie cleared off a space on her editor's desk and unpacked a pastrami sandwich, tuna on white bread, two cream sodas and a bag of barbecue potato chips.

Al Holmstead gazed at the feast benignly—and with no small measure of wistfulness. "Just like old times, huh?" he said.

"Yup. I even told them to use tuna packed in oil."

"And not a thing on this desk that won't kill you."

He picked up the pastrami sandwich with both hands. "Open those chips, will you?"

Aggie did so, scooped up a handful and sat in the chair opposite him. She swung up her booted feet to rest on the corner of his desk and reached for the tuna sandwich.

He glared at her. "I always hated it when you did that," he said, referring to the feet on the desk.

She grinned. "I know." She took a bite out of the sandwich. "So, what do you think?"

He regarded her contemplatively while he chewed, swallowed and took a swig of his soda. "I think," he decided at last, "you ought to watch out for that mayonnaise and all those greasy chips. You're what now? Thirty-six?"

She scowled at him. "Thirty-four."

He gave a small sorrowful shake of his head. "The old biological clock is ticking, babe. And you can't expect to catch a man with hippopotamus hips or clogged arteries."

She returned flatly, "Very funny. See me laugh." Deliberately, she took another bite of the sandwich, enjoyed it thoroughly and then added, "And look who's talking about biological clocks. Yours isn't exactly running backward."

"Yeah, but mine is just counting down to a heart attack. When your alarm goes off, it's goodbye Huggies, hello Soup-for-One—permanently."

Aggie finished chewing slowly, took a long drink from her soda bottle and said, with absolutely no hint of warmth in her voice, "Did anyone ever tell you that any resemblance between you and Lou Grant is purely superficial?"

Their needling each other was routine, and was as

old as their relationship, which was slightly over ten years. Al couldn't know how much that last barb of his had rankled—as it would, Aggie hastily assured herself, any woman over thirty. She decided not to hold his ignorance against him.

Al ate methodically, his elbows resting on the desk, his eyes watching her intently, sizing her up. It was an intimidation technique that had proven quite effective with others; Aggie barely noticed.

"So, what did you think about my article?" she asked again.

"I sure hope you didn't come here looking to have your ego fluffed up. You ought to know better than that by now." He eyed the paper sack from which the sandwiches had come meaningfully. "If there's lemon cream pie in there, though, you just might be a candidate for sainthood."

Aggie closed her hand over the sack. "And if you want to live to find out what's in the sack, you'll tell me what you think of the column."

He took another bite of the sandwich and chewed thoughtfully. "It was an improvement over last week's. 'Woman fends off rapist with hat pin.' Give me a break."

"It happened," she replied.

She held his gaze.

He chewed, swallowed, then said casually, "It was fine. Back to your old form. Reminds me of the old days."

His highest praise.

Aggie put down her sandwich and set her feet on the floor, her tone brisk. "Good. Because I have an idea."

"I didn't think all this was because you liked me."

He gestured toward the food wrappers and potato-chip crumbs that littered his desk.

Aggie grinned. "Don't be so sure."

He finished off the last bite of sandwich and reached for the soda. "So what's your idea? I've got a meeting in ten minutes so I hope it's a small one."

"Medium-size, actually."

Aggie wiped her hands on a paper napkin, then on her jeans. She had never been nervous presenting an idea to Al before, not ever. What was it about the mysterious stranger called Michael that made her feel as though she were walking a tightrope over danger with every breath she took? The excited, fluttering feeling in her stomach had not gone away since the conversation she'd had with him last night. She felt as though she were about to stumble onto something momentous, as though her life was already beginning to entwine with his in some unpredictable pattern. It scared her a little. But it was mostly thrilling.

"I want to follow up on him," she said.

"What? The guy in your column?"

She nodded. "I want to do a kind of miniseries on him, walk him through rediscovering his past, stay with him and see how his future turns out."

Al sipped his soda thoughtfully. "And what if it doesn't turn out? What if he doesn't remember, or what if he turns out to be some kook—an escapee from a mental hospital? That's more than likely, you know. You find out the guy's just another poor slob who slipped through the cracks. What happens to your series then?"

Aggie had thought about that. There was only one answer. "Then I'll write about that," she said. "It's a story worth telling, isn't it? The thousands of homeless wandering the streets, many of them in need of psychiatric care but victims of a system that can't afford to keep them?''

"It's been done." But his eyes were interested.

"It could stand doing again. Besides…" This she had not intended to say, because she had no evidence to support her supposition. But that did not make her any less certain. "I don't think that's his story."

"Oh, yeah? What do you think his story is?"

She hesitated, then shook her head. "I don't know. I wouldn't begin to guess. That's where the hook is, isn't it? For me *and* my readers."

"Maybe," he admitted slowly.

He was obviously intrigued. Aggie could practically see the wheels turning in his head.

Then he added, "But this sounds like a feature to me."

"No." Her voice was a lot sharper than she intended it to be. "You can't do that. I found him—"

"So to speak," Al chided.

"It was my idea, and you can't take him away from me!"

"And you can't dictate to this paper what it will or will not print—any more than I can tell you what to put in your columns. So why'd you come to me with this, anyway?" His tone was mildly admonishing, but more than a little amused.

She glared at him furiously. "Because I had a suspicion you might try something like this, you dirty, low-down, sneaking—"

He held up a hand for silence or surrender. "Hold on there. I haven't done anything yet, low-down, sneaky or otherwise. The truth is, I think more people read your column than ever thought about reading our features, or hard news, for that matter.''

That was typical of Al. Just when she was ready to strangle him, he'd say something like that—knowing full well, no doubt, that it would be considered rude in most circles to throw a half-eaten tuna sandwich at someone who had just given you a compliment.

She very wisely remained silent and bit into the sandwich, chewing with energy. He tapped his fingers against the desk, staring off into the distance, a pose designed for deep thought.

He murmured, '''Lost in Seattle.' I like it. So we stick with this guy, step by step on the road to recovery. You've spent some time with him, right? You're convinced he's on the up-and-up?''

Aggie nodded cautiously, watching him.

He drew his finger through the air, writing invisible copy. ''What's it like to be homeless, mentally ill—''

''No one said he was mentally ill,'' Aggie objected.

He ignored her. ''Dependent on strangers—or worse, on the system—for your very life. Who are you without your past? Without a name, a driver's license, a social security number. Without a memory to tell you what kind of work you used to do or what you'd be good at. How do you earn a living? Who do you turn to? Who's out there to help? Yeah, we could go that way.'' He looked at her. ''Or we could go with a 'Do You Know This Man?' angle. Run his picture, publish the details...''

The last bite of sandwich she had taken lodged heavily somewhere in the center of Aggie's chest. She felt cold. ''Are you sure that would be wise?''

''I'm just surprised nobody else has picked up on it

yet. Those television people would love something like this.''

In Al's opinion, broadcast journalism was one step above supermarket tabloids. His running feud with the major news shows was notorious.

Aggie said carefully, ''Nobody else *knows* about it.''

He ticked off the list on his fingers. ''The paramedics who brought him in, the E.R. personnel, the police, the nurses on his floor, the people who fill out the insurance forms...''

Aggie shook her head impatiently. ''No one at the hospital would release information on a patient without permission, that's cause for dismissal. And the police would check with me before going to the press—if the press was even interested. I mean, come on, Al. Running naked in the woods? Stranger things than that happen in broad daylight in downtown Seattle every day. What makes it interesting is—''

''The amnesia, yes, I know. So why not give this guy a hand? Print his picture, tell the story. You'll have people calling from all over—some of them nuts, it's true, but *somebody* out there has got to know this man. He could have his life back in a matter of days, and we would have done our good deed for the year. Maybe earn yourself a community service award in the process, which is one award I happen to know you do *not* have an excess of.''

Aggie took a drink of her soda, phrasing her thoughts with care. ''What if,'' she offered, ''the people who find him are people he doesn't *want* to find him?''

''Like the FBI?'' Al suggested. ''Now, that would be a story!''

"Like someone who wants to kill him," Aggie snapped. "Like someone he could testify against for what they did to him. Even Russ says there's a possibility he was a kidnapping victim. And we could lead the bad guys right to him—how would you feel about that?"

"Hell of a story," Al mused out loud, but the twinkle in his eyes gave him away just in time.

Aggie sat back in her chair and crossed her arms.

"At least ask him whether or not he wants us to publish his picture," Al suggested. "It's only fair that he have a choice."

"I suppose," Aggie agreed reluctantly. "But it still seems like a dangerous thing to do."

Al's expression turned sly. "Of course," he said, "if we publish his photograph and someone recognizes him right away, that would make for a real short series on the Man Without a Name, wouldn't it? You wouldn't have an ulterior motive for wanting to keep this one under wraps, would you?"

Aggie stared at him defiantly, but she had to swallow back a bitter taste in her mouth. "Don't be ridiculous. I'm not *that* selfish." At least she didn't think she was. "I want to help him. This could be an important series and I owe him a lot for letting me do it."

Al just continued to look at her speculatively. He said nothing. She hated it when he did that.

Finally, he said, "All right, he's all yours. We'll steer clear of a feature for now, but if anything breaks on this guy—I mean, if he should turn out to be the long-lost heir to a Russian throne or a CIA hit man, or something—all bets are off. And I never spoke to you, got it?"

Sheer relief bubbled upward in Aggie and exploded in a grin. "Got it," she assured him.

He was already heading toward the door and the meeting for which he was characteristically late. He grabbed his jacket and shrugged into it. "This was great. Let's do it again sometime."

Aggie took one container of pie from the sack and placed it and a plastic fork on his desk, then she began stuffing food wrappers and leftovers into the sack. "By the way," she said, "it's lemon cream."

He groaned in anticipation. "It had better be here when I get back."

He opened the door.

"And he's not going to turn out to be a Russian prince," she called after him, "or a double agent, either."

His only reply was a dismissive wave, and Aggie turned back to her cleaning up. She added quietly to herself, "He's something a lot stranger than that."

CHAPTER FOUR

"And he gave you permission?" David said, astonished.

"Who? Al?"

"No, the patient. The victim. Michael."

Aggie bristled. "He is not a victim. Not of me, anyway. And of course he gave me permission."

David gave her a glance that was a little too knowing, but didn't reply. Not right away, in any case.

They were having an early dinner at the Canton Empress because David went on duty at the hospital at seven. Seattle boasted hundreds of excellent restaurants of ethnic and gourmet cuisine, and Aggie knew them all. The Canton Empress was a cellar room with plastic tablecloths and fluorescent lighting whose only decoration consisted of a set of tin-plated wind chimes set before a rotating fan. It was one of Aggie's favorite eateries in the city.

"Come on, why are you looking at me that way? What's the problem?" she said.

David put the last of the mandarin beef onto his plate. "You don't think you're exploiting him, just the least bit?"

Aggie put down her fork with a clatter and released an impatient, frustrated sigh. "Is that the kind of person you think I am? Is that the reputation I have in this business? I'm an honest, hardworking journalist—"

"Who has been known to go after a story a little

too hard,'' David pointed out. And before she could launch another attack, added, ''Not that ambition is such a bad thing. That's what got you where you are today.''

''Right,'' Aggie agreed, only slightly mollified. ''Besides, this isn't a story. I'm just trying to help the guy out, okay? It seems the least I can do after knocking him flat with my car. And okay,'' she admitted, squirming a little in her chair. ''So it won't do my career any harm. It's an angle that my readers should find interesting, and it might spin off a few columns. I'll be careful what I say, and I've already promised him he could read everything before it goes to press. I'm not trying to invade anyone's privacy here.''

''Generous of you.''

Aggie looked for sarcasm, but David was too busy finishing off the food. Aggie glanced wryly at her barely touched plate. She had plied two men with food today and hadn't gotten a decent meal for herself between them.

''It's not like I'm trying to deceive anybody,'' she went on. ''It's going to be good for everyone concerned. Don't you think?''

David glanced up. ''You're asking me?''

''Of course I'm asking you!'' she replied, exasperated. ''Why else would I be buying you dinner?''

''Ah.'' He nodded thoughtfully, refilling his small teacup from the pot, and then warming hers. ''A bribe.''

She did not dignify that remark with a reply, turning her attention instead to her now-cold portion of sweet-and-sour pork.

''I see just one problem,'' he said after a moment, sipping his tea. ''Well, two. The first is that his memory could return at any minute—tonight, tomorrow or next Wednesday—and when it does, he's going to go back to his pregnant wife and half-million-dollar town house and cushy corporate vice presidency, leaving you high and dry for a column.''

The remark about the pregnant wife did not bother her; after all, it wasn't as though she had any *romantic* interest in the mysterious Michael. Still, it unsettled her a little because until that moment, she hadn't really imagined that he might be married, with a family who was looking for him, waiting for him…and it was odd that she had not thought this was a possibility. Even now, when she tried to picture it, she found the idea just didn't suit him. A family man? She didn't think so.

What she found even more interesting was that when David spun out a fictional life for Michael, he added many of the same elements she did—wealth, power, sophistication. They were both obviously picking up on some subtle signals from him that formed a definitive profile. But the profile couldn't be all that accurate; people who lived in half-million-dollar town houses and drove Porsches—she added that touch— didn't go missing without someone noticing. Neither did people who left behind pregnant wives.

David continued, ''And the second problem is, how are you going to keep up with him? I mean, the poor guy has got enough problems trying to put his life back together. He can't accommodate your schedule while he's trying to find a bed at the mission or scrounge up a hot meal. The truth is, I think it's a great idea, but I don't see how you can expect to give a week-by-week progress report on him when you might not be able to find him by the second week.''

Aggie grew very busy with her almond chicken. "Actually, I'll know exactly where to find him."

"Oh, yeah?" David looked interested. "Did you find him a place to stay?"

"That's right."

"Where?"

She put down her fork, touched a napkin to her lips and looked at him. "With me."

The words were barely out of her mouth, before David began shaking his head. "Oh, no, I don't think so. Not a chance. You've done some crazy things in your life, but you can just forget about adding this one to your list. No way in this world."

She waited patiently for him to finish and then she picked up her fork again. "I wasn't asking your permission, David."

"And you're not getting it, either! Come on, Aggie, are you serious? Are you seriously considering taking this perfect stranger into your home? All alone out there in Idlewood—"

"You make it sound like a remote sheep station in Australia. We're perfectly civilized in the suburbs now. We have cable TV and running water and access to 911 and everything."

He ignored her, leaning forward with an intensely stubborn look on his face. "The point is, you know nothing about him. Literally, nothing. Do the words *no references* mean anything to you? This is insane! And speaking of insane, the chances are better than average, given the circumstances under which you found him, that this man has serious psychiatric problems. He may be a danger to himself or to society. If you think I'm going to let you—"

"Then why are you releasing him?"

David blinked. "What?"

"If you think he's such a danger to society, why are you releasing him from the hospital tomorrow?"

He looked uncomfortable. "You know that's not my decision to make. I work the trauma team, I'm not even the attending physician."

"But if you were, you wouldn't keep him hospitalized, would you?"

He shifted uneasily. "We're a private hospital. We have rules we have to operate under. Whether or not they might be the best rules isn't part of this discussion."

Aggie took some satisfaction in noting that he had completely lost interest in his meal, what little of it remained. She said calmly, "And the fact is, if it weren't for your rules, he wouldn't need to come home with me because you would keep him hospitalized until you were sure he could take care of himself, wouldn't you?"

David's lips tightened. "If it were my choice, yes."

Aggie relaxed her expression into one of gentle persuasion. "David, you know this is the right thing to do. The moral and humane thing to do."

"It's crazy," David responded shortly. But she could see defeat begin to register in his eyes. "He could be a convicted felon, a rapist or a child molester—"

"The police haven't found anything on him. I checked."

"That doesn't mean he's not a serial killer. That just means he doesn't have a police record—in Washington State."

"Oh, come on, David." Her exasperation was beginning to show. "If I apply those criteria to my life, everyone I ever meet could be a serial killer. What am I going to do, never meet anyone again?''

''You don't have to take everyone you meet home to live with you!''

She stared at him. He stared back.

Finally, he said, ''You're not going to change your mind, are you?''

''He can have my office, it's got its own dead bolt, and everything. All my neighbors are within shouting distance. I'm well trained in self-defense. And despite what you may think, I'm not as stupid as I look. At the first sign of anything funny, he's out of there. Besides, can you look me in the eye and honestly tell me you think he's dangerous?''

David chose to be stubborn. ''I can't tell you he's not.''

She sighed and rolled her eyes.

''And I can't tell you what to do,'' he admitted at last, shoulders slumping. ''So be careful. I'll be checking with you daily,'' he added by way of warning.

''Why not hourly?'' But Aggie was relieved. She might not have her brother's approval, but at least he wasn't angry.

Aggie took another bite of the dinner, and put down the fork. There was just one more thing she needed to ask. ''By the way,'' she said as casually as possible, ''how did his blood work turn out?''

''What?'' David was frowning into his cup of tea and he looked up, distracted. ''Oh—fine. Except for a bump on the head, he seems to be a perfectly normal male. HIV negative, if that's what you're asking.''

She bristled. ''Thanks, but that was *not* what I was asking, and I resent the implication.'' Then she made herself relax and, before he could interrupt again, she added lightly, "So he is human, after all, huh?"

For a moment he didn't seem to remember to what she was referring, then he laughed. "Oh, yeah—the screw-up at the lab. Yeah." And the amusement faded into ruefulness. "I guess the one thing we *do* know about him is that he's human."

Aggie smiled again and lifted her own teacup, a little ashamed of the relief she felt.

"Right," she agreed. "At least that's one thing."

Michael awoke with his heart racing and the remnants of a dream falling into tatters around him. Running…yes, running with the wind in his hair and the spring of the earth beneath his feet, the moon darting in and out of a ragged network of clouds, the thrill of the chase and the taste of fear…but was he being chased, or was it he who was doing the chasing?

He lifted a hand to push back his hair from his damp face and then stopped, staring at the appendage that should have been his, too shocked to even feel horror. His hand. It wasn't his hand…and it was. Its shape was elongated, deformed, fingers withered and topped with claws, the top of it covered with thick silver-brown hair, the palm rough and dark. It was hideous. It was curiously enthralling. It was the hand of a monster.

"Good evening, Michael."

The door swung open to admit a cheerful nurse with a tray holding plastic-domed dishes. He ducked his hand under the sheet, his heart pounding.

"Supper's a little late tonight. I hope you're not starved."

She swung the bed table over the bed and pushed a

button that raised his head and shoulders. She removed the plastic dome from the center dish and the paper covering from the glass of juice. "Fried chicken tonight. It's not bad. I had it earlier in the cafeteria. Can I get anything else for you right now?"

Michael wanted to sweep the tray off the table and onto the floor; he wanted to roar at her and send her stumbling for the door. Instead, he forced himself to smile and hoped she didn't notice how shaky it was.

"Thank you," he said. "It looks good."

"I'll be back in a little while, then." She flashed a flirtatious grin at him as she departed. "Be sure to clean your plate. I'll check."

Michael sat stiff and straight when she was gone, breathing slowly, trying to calm his heartbeat and clear his mind. Neither effort was successful. Slowly, with a dread compulsion he couldn't control, he pulled his hand out from under the sheet.

It was perfectly normal.

A few scratches, a few freckles, a fine sprinkling of pale hair on the back...a perfectly normal, human hand.

Michael released a long unsteady breath and sank back against the pillows, perspiration trickling down his face. A trick of his eyes, that was all. It was over. He was perfectly normal.

But it was a long time before he felt normal. And he did not eat at all that night.

Castle St. Clare, Alaska

It was a massive structure, built into the side of a mountain that was older than Time, carved of native stone and constructed so cleverly that it seemed not to be built on the mountain at all; rather, it was a part of it, a natural outgrowth of the rock face itself. It was old. It had been old when the first czars had ruled, old when the first icebreakers had plowed through the stormy Arctic sea, old when the grand stone fortresses of which the Europeans were so proud lined the Valley Loire. Winds had screamed and torn at it, rain and snow and ice had battered it, killing cold and baking sun had smoothed its outer surface to a high-polished sheen. But the occupants inside remained untouched by the outside world. It was a fortress, a haven. A safe house.

Accessible only by air even in good weather, few people from the outside even knew of its existence. Those who did did not require much persuasion to give it a wide berth. Castle St. Clare was a private place, a refuge, and no one was welcome there who did not belong.

Though it was built like a fortress and perfectly capable of withstanding any disaster, whether man-made or natural, inside it offered every comfort, along with a level of luxury available to only a privileged few anywhere in the world. The St. Clares were among the privileged. Centuries of ambition, determination and dedication to triumph had put Monets and Raphaels on the wall, Aubusson on the floors, Baccarat crystal on the table. But if one looked closely, it was possible to discern a certain dissonance between the elegance of the furnishings and the architecture of the house.

The delicate Queen Anne furniture and porcelain vases warred with the massive, smoke-scarred stone walls and rough-hewn crossbeams. Breathtakingly sculptured marble mantelpieces looked out of place over walk-in fireplaces that were big enough to burn an entire tree—and had done so, in the days before self-contained electric generators and underground fuel storage tanks. There were gilt-framed mirrors and gun ports, hand-sculpted moldings and security cameras. This was a house built to endure, furnished with elegance and style, but the evidence of its origins lingered around every corner, behind each door and up every staircase. Those who lived there knew the consequences of power and never forgot that they might one day be called upon to defend it again as their ancestors had done in the dim and distant past.

There were forty-three bedrooms. Some were no more than cubbyholes deep within the warrenlike network of corridors that ran beneath the mountain; others were modern, comfortable suites with Jacuzzis, shower rooms and home gyms. At any one time, approximately one third of the rooms were filled. When the entire clan gathered, the huge house bulged at the seams and adjacent properties were opened up, for Castle St. Clare was home base to almost one hundred families scattered throughout the world.

The head of this proud empire was Sebastian St. Clare, a big man of indeterminate age and unquestioned authority. He had a magnificent mane of flowing white hair, piercing blue eyes and a voice, when in form, that could shake the very foundation of the castle itself. His voice was in just such form now, and so was his mood.

Sebastian St. Clare listened in powerful silence until the voice on the other end of the telephone completed its tale. Then he said, in a growl so low and so intense that it reverberated through the stone floors, ''What do you mean, *you lost him?*''

In a second-floor room of the Holiday Inn just outside of Seattle, Noel Duprey winced and held the receiver away from his ear a few inches. When he thought it was safe to speak again, he said, "I'm sorry, *Grand-père*." He used the formal mode of address more out of respect than because relationship gave him the right. "I don't know how it happened."

On the other end of the line, Sebastian let his temper pass and considered the situation. "Gavin is the best tracker we have," he said eventually, thinking out loud. "He hasn't picked up a trace?"

"Not that I can tell, sir."

"Let me speak to him," Sebastian demanded impatiently.

Noel glanced toward a darkened corner of the room, where the shape of his companion, curled in a ball and fast asleep, could barely be discerned. "Gavin is... indisposed at the moment," he said wryly. "He had a rough night."

Sebastian grunted in reply.

"As a matter of fact," Noel went on, lowering his voice confidentially, "Gavin is becoming something of a problem. He's never been entirely stable and it seems to me he's getting worse. I'm not sure he should have been allowed to come along."

"You're not, are you?"

They both knew there was insanity in Gavin's line, a defective gene that had produced the first renegade in the St. Clare dynasty in almost three hundred years. It was a shame, and it wasn't Gavin's fault; still, he was becoming a problem.

Noel suspected he was on the verge of overstepping his bounds, but he glanced toward the corner, continued to keep his voice low and added, "I just think I could have done better on my own. We almost had him, you know. But Gavin went after him in full attack—''

"Was he hurt?"

Sebastian's voice was harsh with alarm, and Noel did not have to wonder who the old man's concern was for.

"He hardly got near our quarry. But Gavin got his ear slashed and sustained a pretty bad puncture on his arm. By the time he finished nursing his wounds, the trail was cold. It rains a lot here,'' he added, with an aesthete's distaste for discomfort.

"Let me tell you something,'' Sebastian said. "You wouldn't have gotten this far without Gavin. Whatever else he is, he's good at what he does, and you couldn't track your way out of a subway station. Your orders are to stay there until you find him, do you understand that?''

Then he added, because a good leader never failed to give encouragement when it was needed and praise when it was deserved, "What you lack in tracking instinct, you make up for in brains. We can lose all our other weapons, but no one can take from us our ability to think. No one can take our reason unless we surrender it voluntarily. Don't you ever forget that, Noel.''

Noel replied quietly, "No, sir.''

"Now use your brain, damn it.'' Sebastian's voice gruffened with emotion. "Find my heir. Bring him home to me.''

He hung up the phone without waiting for a reply. There was nothing else to be said.

The orders of Sebastian St. Clare were never disobeyed. They would return the prodigal to him.

If they were able.

If there was anything left of him to return.

CHAPTER FIVE

Michael left the hospital at ten o'clock in the morning wearing a pair of new jeans, a white cotton shirt with the sleeves rolled up, the appropriate underwear and a pair of running shoes. The clothing was a gift from the nurses on the floor, and they seemed to enjoy the exchange of good-natured banter he initiated when they presented the outfit to him. Michael was appreciative, but he was now worried, for the first time, about money. He had a feeling he was not accustomed to doing that.

He had not told anyone about his hallucination, and it hadn't happened again.

"The first thing we'll do," Aggie said briskly as they left the smells of alcohol and ammonia for the rain-fresh air of the world outside, "is make the rounds of all the government agencies. The health department, employment department, county assistance…" She ticked off the list on her fingers. "Then we'll try the established services, like United Way and Red Cross and Salvation Army. There are facilities out there to help you. All that remains to be seen is how well they work."

He glanced at her in amusement. "Do you always have a plan, Aggie McDonald?"

Her car was parked in the patient loading zone. She said, "Of course," and opened the passenger-side door for him.

Michael got in, absently fingering the medallion

around his neck. He wondered how much it might bring if he sold it.

"The first thing we have to do," Aggie continued as she slid into the driver's seat, "is make a list of priorities. What is it that you need? Health care, food stamps, job training? Supplemental income, housing?"

He murmured, "How about all of the above?"

She was wearing a cotton dress with sunflowers on it and canvas shoes. The dress came to her calves, but she had left the buttons undone from hem to knee and when she moved, the material fluttered around her legs in an enchanting manner. Yellow suited her.

She backed out of the parking space. "Well, of course. But the point is to approach all this systematically. I had another idea, too, and this might be your best bet. Maybe we could spend the next few days trying to find out what you're good at—they say some learned skills never really go away, you know—and then I'll describe your aptitudes in my column. I wouldn't be a bit surprised if someone out there had a job for you."

"You changed your shampoo," he said.

She cast him a laughing, startled look. He noticed for the first time she had freckles across her nose, and her eyes, in the natural light of day, sparkled like sunbeams on water.

"I've been staying at my brother's place," she said. "I used his shampoo... You're amazing."

"Thank you."

He could have told her other things—that her hands had recently been in dish soap, that she had been inside a shop that baked bread, that she had stopped at a self-service gas station before coming to the hospital.

But it seemed irrelevant. He much preferred to watch her face, so mobile and expressive, as she talked.

But his gaze seemed to make her uncomfortable, because when she took her eyes off the road long enough to glance at him, she looked away immediately, and said, "Listen, there's something we should talk about."

"All right."

He rested one elbow on the back of the seat and turned toward her as much as the seat belt would allow. She kept her eyes on the road.

"While I'm making all these grandiose plans to help you put your life back together," she said, with just the faintest trace of self-mockery in her tone, "I should probably mention that there's one very simple thing we could do that might solve your problem completely. My editor said he would run your picture in the paper—with a feature—if you wanted. There must be people who know you here. If they saw your picture in the paper, all they would have to do is call. We could give a photo to the television stations, too," she added reluctantly. "But my boss would want the exclusive for at least a day. It's only fair."

She cast him a look that was oddly anxious. "Well? What do you think?"

He continued to look at her, but what he saw was far away...the view from a high window. Traffic below, taxicabs, another building across from him, its opaque windows staring like the eyes of the dead...

"I don't think I'm from here," he said slowly. "No one would know me here."

She darted another quick glance at him. "Are you sure?"

A limousine, a bridge, a familiar view...

"New York," he said, his eyes focusing on her abruptly. "That's where I'm from. No," he corrected himself with a quick, instinctive shake of his head. "Not from. I worked there. My office was there. But I'm from…" His vision clouded again, as did his mind, as the brief ray of memory that had peeked through was once again swallowed by thunderheads. "Somewhere else," he finished simply.

"Michael, that's wonderful!" She tossed a jubilant look at him and took her hand off the steering wheel to squeeze his. "You've remembered something. I knew it would come back to you. It may take a little while, but you'll get your memory back, I just know it! Bits and pieces, that's all it takes, then we just put the pieces together. You remembered where you worked.

"Of course," she added practically, and some of the elation left her tone, "New York is a big city. I don't suppose you could narrow it down?"

He smiled, looking at her hand, which still enclosed his. He liked the feel of that. Warm and encouraging, and…human.

"No," he answered. "I'm afraid not. Not at the moment, anyway."

"Well." She gave his hand an extra squeeze, and then left it. "It'll come back. I'm sure of it. Meanwhile, this is definitely a good sign."

Her expression grew thoughtful as she negotiated the traffic downtown and headed for the ferry. "You worked in New York," she repeated. "So what brought you to Seattle? Business? Of course, it had to be business. And if it was, you would have to know people here."

She gave him that look again, quick, uncertain, anxious. "This really might be the answer, Michael. It would explain why no one has filed a missing person's report on you, why your family isn't frantic...Who knows how long you had planned to be away? It could take days for whoever you were supposed to meet with here to realize something is wrong and get in touch with the authorities. But if we published your picture—"

"No," he said immediately.

He could tell from the way her shoulders relaxed against the seat that that was the right answer. Her reaction only confirmed what he felt, although he couldn't explain it: putting his picture in the paper would be very dangerous.

He didn't want to be found that badly. Maybe he didn't want to be found at all.

He realized she had looked at him again, as though waiting for an explanation. He didn't have one. At least, he didn't have one he was ready to share with her.

He said, "I just don't think it would be a good idea."

Aggie nodded. "Me, neither. We don't know what happened to you before...well, before. And we don't know what—or who—we might be sending you back to if we publish your picture. It just seems irresponsible to me. I say until we know more, we go for the anonymity angle."

He smiled, amazed by her easy grasp of the situation. It had crossed his mind more than once since the accident to wonder how he would be able to tell who, among all the strangers who surrounded him, he could trust. Now he knew. He could trust Aggie McDonald. He didn't need anyone else.

When she pulled onto the ferry ramp, he said, "We're leaving the city? Where are we going?"

She had told him she would arrange a place for him to stay and he hadn't questioned her any further. It did not matter to him what kind of place it was, because he didn't intend to be there long. The same intuition that told him it would be dangerous to publicize his photograph also insisted he would be foolish to stay in Seattle where anyone might be looking for him. He had seen no reason to voice his concerns to Aggie, however, who had been so generous with her concern. All he needed was a few days to orient himself and decide where to go from here, all he asked was a roof over his head. But he had expected that roof to be in the city.

Aggie guided her car into a parking spot before answering, "Home. We're going home."

She turned off the ignition, pocketed the keys and suggested, "Let's get out. It's a twenty-minute ride and the morning's too nice to stay inside."

Her voice was pleasant and her smile was open, but her body language practically shouted that she was keeping something from him. He watched her carefully as she got out of the car, and in a moment he did the same.

The breeze caught his hair and tossed it around his shoulders; it tasted of the sea and felt good on his skin. Michael combed back his hair with his fingers, aware of the curious stares of other passengers as he walked with Aggie toward the railing.

Aggie noticed, too, and she smiled at him. "You're a striking-looking man," she told him. "I'm sure you get stares wherever you go."

Michael frowned. "I'm not so sure that's a good thing."

She sobered. "Maybe not."

They found a place against the railing. He looked down at her. "Where are we going, Aggie?"

She leaned back, with both elbows on the railing, pretending casualness and confidence. Again, he sensed the opposite.

"I've decided you should stay with me," she said. "My office is next to my house—it's not very elegant, but it's got a sleeper sofa and a bathroom and even a coffeemaker. You'll like it, it's right on the water. And it'll give you privacy, a chance to recuperate. It's the perfect solution."

The engines throbbed, and the ferry started to pull away from the dock. The wind tugged at Michael's hair with increased vigor. "You should have told me," he said.

She was defensive. "Why?"

"I'm not sure this is a good idea."

"You have a better one?"

"You don't know anything about me. *I* don't know anything about me. I don't want to be held responsible if—"

If what? He couldn't finish the sentence, and the unspoken possibilities hung in the air between them.

Her light tone was unconvincing. "I promise not to hold you responsible if you murder me in my sleep."

He didn't smile. She looked away.

"All right," she said, somewhat stiffly. "I read the papers. I know the kinds of maniacs that are running loose. But I don't think you're one of them."

"How can you be sure?"

There was certainty in her eyes, doubt in her face. He wished he could be even that confident.

"For one thing," she said, "I don't think a maniac would be so concerned about responsibility."

An errant ray of sun flashed fire in her hair, and then wind plastered her dress to her body. Flat stomach, shapely thighs. Dancing red hair. And a world full of the scent of her. An unleashed part of his mind played with the fantasy of drawing her close and inhaling deeply of her, burying himself in the scent of her, drowning in it… And he could see that she was not completely oblivious to those undercurrents. She shifted position against the railing, subtly moving away from him.

He said, "I make you nervous."

He could see the movement of her throat muscles as she swallowed. He thought about tracing the slim ridged column with his tongue. Delicious.

"A little. Yes."

"Perhaps you should listen to your instincts," he said softly.

Aggie turned her face toward his. Their eyes met and held, and for a moment there was no one on the ferry but the two of them, nothing in the world but the moment that hung silent and suspended between them: no wind, no sea, no thrumming engines. Just Aggie. Just Michael. Danger. Possibilities. Promises of discovery that quivered between them. The excitement of the unknown. Courage. Uncertainty. Acceptance.

"What do your instincts tell you, Michael?"

He lifted his hand, let his fingers drift through a feathering of hair that the wind had parted near her forehead. She didn't flinch, though he thought she might.

"About you?"

She answered, "About you."

He dropped his hand, holding her only with his eyes. And he replied soberly only what he knew to be the truth. "That you should be careful, Aggie McDonald."

He turned then and leaned his elbows on the railing as she had done, standing in profile to her, not touching yet filled with her, still. After a moment, she did the same.

The ferry ride took twenty minutes. It was slightly longer than the route Aggie generally took, but she was not yet ready to face that lonely stretch of road where the accident had occurred. On the other hand, perhaps she was being unfair to Michael. Perhaps returning to the scene of the accident would trigger something in his memory.

She asked him about it as they drove off the ramp and turned left onto a state road. "I could circle around," she volunteered, "and go back that way. It would take about half an hour."

"Maybe another time."

He was polite, distant. The enormous sexual energy she had sensed from him on the ferry was now completely in check, drawn tightly within himself and under control, but not gone. It would never be completely gone for a man like Michael.

She said, giving him a quick sideways glance, "I should have asked you before, but it seemed kind of pointless under the circumstances. I don't suppose you remember whether or not there was a dog with you that night?"

Michael frowned. Flash: *Himself, whirling to face a*

man with long white hair, and shouting, "You can't ask this of me! I've spent my life trying not to be like you, you know that's true! You can't..." And in the background an animal—a dog?—pacing, whining anxiously.

"Michael?"

He shook his head, and the memory evaporated like mist. "No," he said. "I don't remember a dog."

Aggie knew he was lying, but she didn't want to press. In fact, she felt strongly that she had already stepped dangerously close to some invisible boundary today, and decided a neutral topic would be the best course.

"Don't expect too much until you see the place," she chatted easily. "I'm a pretty sloppy worker, and I haven't been home to straighten up the office. I thought I'd just leave the office equipment there, if it won't be in your way, and work on my laptop for the next few weeks. Of course, I might have to disturb you now and then for the fax machine or printer, but for the most part you'll have the place to yourself. The office has its own phone line, too."

He nodded and murmured appropriate responses occasionally, but Aggie sensed he wasn't really listening, which suited her fine. She kept up the harmless, meaningless chatter all the way home.

Home was a tiny brick building, vaguely Georgian in architecture, with dormer attic windows and two flagstone patios. There were flower beds with pansies and a stained-glass fanlight over the front door. The front yard was a handkerchief-size square of green lawn; the backyard was Spirit Lake. In between the two and to the east of the main house was a small brick garage that she had converted into her office.

She left the car in the circular driveway and said, "Do you want to come in and look around? We can go through the house to the office, and I'll show you where you'll be staying. I'll have to get some linens, too, for your bed. Are you hungry?"

There was an amused spark in his eye as he followed her onto the small front porch. "You don't have to fuss," he told her. "And you don't have to keep talking to keep me entertained."

She unlocked the door with an apologetic shrug. "I guess I was chattering," she admitted. "It's an old interview trick I used to use to put people at ease. Guess it's not working too well, huh?"

He smiled at her. "I'm at ease," he told her.

Aggie could not imagine a situation in which he wouldn't be.

She opened the door and gestured him inside, making a quick sweep behind him to pick up discarded articles of clothing, stray magazines and soft-drink cans. "Like I said," she apologized, "I haven't had a chance to straighten up."

He looked around with genuine appreciation. "This is charming."

It was designed like a miniature mansion, with *miniature* being the key word. The floors were gleaming hardwood, the fireplace faux marble. The three-foot foyer was tiled in slate and overhung by a crystal chandelier. The built-in bookcases on either side of the fireplace in the living room hid an entertainment center and displayed Aggie's collection of trophies and awards, as well as her few precious pieces of crystal and china. The furniture was scaled to the room—a curved love seat, two slender chairs and delicate lamp tables were drawn up around a pale blue and ivory rug depicting a rose garden. Palladian windows framed the silver lake on one side, and the pansy beds on the other. The room was filled with light, and one hardly noticed its cramped proportions.

"It has only two bedrooms," Aggie said. "I use one for a library."

Pocket doors led to a room that was lined with books, floor to ceiling, on all four walls. With the shelves added, there was only room for a comfortably plump chair and hassock in the center of the floor, with a small table and floor lamp beside them. The room was painted a deep forest green lacquer, with the colorful contrast of book spines and the faded red paisley chair adding warmth and character. Michael laughed out loud with pleasure when he saw it.

"This is marvelous!" he exclaimed. "A den deep in the forest where nothing can intrude. It's like something out of 'Hansel and Gretel.'"

She grinned, pleased. "I think so, too. And it's good to see you remember your fairy tales."

"Enough to know I didn't care for them much. It seems to me the Big Bad Wolf received far too much of the blame for stupid children's mistakes."

Aggie laughed as she turned from the room. "That's an interesting way of looking at it. My bedroom is over there," she said, gesturing in its direction. "It has French doors with a patio overlooking the lake."

She did not offer to include her bedroom on the tour. There was a limit to hospitality, after all, and she didn't know him *that* well...or trust him that much.

She turned instead toward the small formal dining room with its teardrop chandelier and polished cherry-wood table, which, when surrounded by four chairs, barely left room for one person to walk around. She pushed through the swinging doors to the kitchen, which was wall-to-wall with cabinets and built-in appliances, but managed to leave room for a two-person breakfast nook squeezed into a tiny bay window.

"This is delightful," he said, eyes dancing as he looked around. "Like a dollhouse."

It was a dollhouse, of course, which was the only way Aggie could afford such an expensive neighborhood; the house was much too small for the average family, or even for a couple. But she must have grown used to its dimensions over the past year because until Michael entered it, filling every nook and cranny with his powerful masculine presence, she had never noticed just *how* small.

She had had other men here before. Tall men, big men, sexy men. None of them had ever made her feel quite this crowded.

She moved quickly to the back door—three steps— and opened it. "This is the other patio. It wraps around to the dining room, too, see? And there's the lake— and your guest quarters."

Spirit Lake was one of the myriad bodies of water that defined this part of the state, not impressive by Seattle standards but more than enough for Aggie's needs. Geographically, it was little more than a wide spot in the Green River, but its heavily tree-lined shores and relative isolation made it seem as vast as Elliot Bay and as remote as Alaska.

The lake was, of course, rimmed with houses, some of them designer log cabins meant as summer homes, others elaborate enough to be called estates, but Aggie rarely saw or heard the people who owned them. What she did hear, when she opened her windows at night or on summer afternoons in the office, was the gentle, continual lap of water, the chirp of crickets, the occasional faraway call of a loon. She had fallen in love with the lake first. The house was a bonus.

Michael stood beside her, silent in absorption as he took in the view. His face was composed and relaxed with pleasure, his expression faraway.

Aggie felt a tingle of excitement, for she knew he was remembering something. She said softly, hesitant to break the spell, "Something?"

"It reminds me of a place," he murmured. "Childhood. There were high mountains around us, the smell of the lake...we chased butterflies."

Aggie slipped her hands around his arm, squeezing briefly. "I told you the memories would come. This is great."

"Yes." And he brought his attention back to her with a smile. "I only wish all the memories were as pleasant."

Aggie didn't want to break the mood, but the interviewer in her took over. "What do you mean?" Letting her hands drop from his arm, she gestured him down the flagstone path toward the office. "What bad memories have you had?"

He bent to snap off a stem of lavender that lined the path. The sweet, soft aroma drifted to her as he brought it to his face and inhaled deeply, then drew the stem lightly beneath her chin, tickling. She laughed and pulled away. Sun sparks of contentment played in his eyes.

"I refuse to discuss anything unpleasant at this moment. Wait until the thunder crashes and the rain pours, then ask me again. What's the name of the lake?"

"Spirit Lake."

"I'll bet there's a fascinating legend attached to that."

"If so, I've never heard it. I think it's called that because of the way the mist forms in the early morning, it looks like ghosts dancing on the water. And also because of the sounds the loons make way back in the woods. It can be pretty spooky."

She opened the door to the brick cottage that served as her office.

Unlike any room in the house, the office—no matter what its original purpose had been—was sufficiently spacious to serve its present function. It was decorated with bright, homey colors against white enamel walls: yellow chintz curtains and bright red and blue cushions on the sofa, a copper pot with dried flowers in one corner, a twig cocktail table painted green. A crazy-quilt afghan in colors of purple, green, blue and yellow was folded on the back of an easy chair adjacent to the sofa. Rag rugs were splashes of color on the painted wooden floor.

There was a computer workstation which, Aggie noted with relief, wasn't nearly as messy as she usually left it, and next to it a file cabinet upon which colorful refrigerator magnets held numerous important memos, some of them two years old. A combination telephone/fax machine occupied a corner of the desk, and above the desk were three long shelves of books, some of them reference books, many of them fiction.

Michael stood before the bookshelves, examining the titles without touching them. "Mysteries, science fiction..." He lifted an eyebrow. "Not what I'd expect in a newspaperwoman's office."

She shrugged. "Sometimes I get blocked. It helps to read."

She had been spending a lot more time reading than writing lately, it was true. But she had a feeling those days were over.

"Help yourself to anything that sounds interesting," she added.

He reached for a black notebook-style binder labeled 1989-91. "Even this?"

"Oh." She half moved as though to take it from him, then stopped, feeling foolish. "Those are just my old columns."

Most of Seattle had read them; why shouldn't he? It was silly to feel self-conscious, as though, by reading the columns, he might see more of her than she was prepared to reveal.

He glanced at her with eyes that were quick and perceptive, sensing her inexplicable discomfort as though she had shouted it at him. He put the binder back on the shelf. "Perhaps later," he said. "Though I would like to read them, if you don't mind."

Then she *did* feel foolish. "Of course I don't mind. I'm going to be writing about you. You have every right to decide for yourself whether I'm any good or not."

His eyes smiled at her. "That's not why I want to read them."

She was nervous again. She turned, gesturing to the opposite side of the room, where a wet bar was set up. "There's a little refrigerator stocked with soft drinks, snacks in the cabinets underneath, coffeemaker... I discovered I was spending far too much time running to the house for something to drink, and every time I got there, I'd find a dozen things I'd rather be doing than writing. The snack bar eliminated that problem.

The bathroom is behind that door there. It's kind of small.''

He laughed. "Already I feel guilty. I have more space in this one room than you do in your entire house."

She grinned. "Come to think of it, you're probably right. The sofa folds out into a bed. No one's ever used it, so I can't say how comfortable it is. All you have to do is move that table to the side, there should be plenty of room. I'll bring down towels and sheets as soon as I do a load of laundry."

He turned to her, his expression sober. "Why are you doing this for me, Aggie McDonald?"

She was tempted to be flip, to cite the favor he was doing her by letting her write about him in her column, to shrug it off with a saintly smile. But his eyes held her and they were eyes that wouldn't let her lie.

"I robbed you of your past. The least I can do is give you a place to stay," she said simply.

He went to the open door and stood there, looking out over the lake for a time. When he turned back to her, his smile was a mixture of peace and contentment, sadness and longing.

"Aggie," he said, "this place..." And he made a small gesture with his wrist to include the room, the lake, the lavender-lined path, the house beyond. "It's like something I might once have dreamed of but thought I couldn't have. It's almost as though..." And here he frowned, searching for words. "I was searching for it somehow, when I ran away... Not this place, of course, but one similar to it. It feels good and right to me, and I thank you from the bottom of my heart for offering it to me. But I don't want to be the cause of your guilt."

Aggie shook her head. "I can't help it. I feel guilty. I keep thinking what it would be like if it were me, how it must be to lose your friends, your family, your home, your memories of good times, the lessons you've learned... Those are the things that make you who you are. To lose them is to lose your identity."

A shadow passed over Michael's face, and he looked away. "Perhaps," he said, "in some cases, that isn't such a bad thing."

Aggie shook her head again. "Not for you," she said. "Whoever you are, whatever you lost, that's a good thing. You deserve to have your past back."

His smile was a little slow in coming. "You may be right."

She came toward him a little hesitantly. "Michael, what did you mean when you said, 'When I ran away'?"

He focused on her again. "What? Did I say that?"

She nodded. "Just now."

His eyebrows came together in a moment of concentration and frustration. "I don't know," he admitted at last. "I don't know what I meant."

She patted his arm in reassurance. "That's okay. I mean, that's good. I think if things just keep slipping out like that, eventually we'll be able to form a pattern of some sort."

He smiled down at her. "You are an extraordinary woman," he said.

They were standing very close in the doorway, so close that she could see the sunlight playing through the individual strands of his shot-silver hair, see the bronzed satin texture of his skin, feel the brush of his thigh. So close that the intensity of his rich blue gaze made her heart beat faster, and she lowered her eyes briefly, just enough to break the contact.

"Well," she said with a bright smile, "I think I'll go start lunch. I'm getting hungry, aren't you?"

A playful spark came into his eyes. "Uh-huh." He continued to look at her, teasing now, challenging. And he did not shift his position, even when she glanced past him to indicate she wanted to get by.

"I'll go make us sandwiches, if that's okay. And then I need to make a quick run to the grocery store…"

With another casual pat on his arm, she started to brush past him, but he caught her arms lightly, turning her toward him. Her heart caught in her throat as a half-dozen crazy cascading thoughts tumbled through her mind—the gentle strength of his fingers wrapped around her arms, the clean, warm smell of him, the power of his eyes and the light that leaped there when he looked at her, and insanely, what it would be like to be swept up in his heat and lean, hard strength, lost in his taste.

It seemed an eternity that she was held there, suspended by nothing more than the sheer force of his sensuality, her head tilted back, her lips parted on a caught breath. In fact, it was no time at all, only the time it took for her to realize what a very, very dangerous man he could be.

At that moment, he smiled, and lifted his hand. Her muscles weakened instinctively in anticipation of his touch. But all he did was tuck the sprig of lavender behind her ear and stepped away.

Aggie took a quick steadying breath and continued her monologue as though it had never been interrupted. As though something quite fundamental had not been shaken between her last word and this one. "You should be thinking about the things you need— toiletries and stuff—and I'll pick them up for you while I'm out. There's no need for you to go with me, I'm sure you're tired. You should rest this afternoon. I thought we'd cook out this evening. How do you like your steak?"

His teeth flashed in a grin that was both playful and predatory, amused and teasing. "Rare," he said. "Very rare."

She gave him a quick bright smile, nodded and left quickly. But the smile faded into pensiveness as she walked back toward the house.

"Somehow," she murmured to herself as she left him, "that doesn't surprise me."

CHAPTER SIX

Aggie lit the citronella torches that surrounded the patio and put a festive cloth on the outdoor table. She and Michael had dinner as the sun produced a spectacular display of silver, orange and gold on the ripples of the lake, and Aggie couldn't get over the feeling, absurd as it was, that she was on a date.

She liked to cook; it was one of her weaknesses. She told herself she went to extra trouble, garnishing the salad with red pepper and mandarin orange slices, marinating the steak for four hours, soaking the potatoes in beer before she baked them and making the dinner rolls from scratch, because she enjoyed it, it was fun and she liked good food. All of that was true. But it was also true that most of the pleasure in preparing a good meal was sharing it with someone who admired you for it.

Michael did not disappoint her.

She opened the burgundy that her brother had given her for her birthday—what was she saving it for, anyway?—and enjoyed the light of appreciation in his eyes as he tasted it. "You surprise me," he said. "All these domestic qualities...somehow they don't exactly reflect the woman who wrote those columns I've been reading."

Aggie lifted a shoulder, trying not to feel self-conscious. "Maybe you should read further."

"Or read between the lines." He smiled at her. "I intend to."

Aggie speared her salad. "You should be careful about drawing conclusions from surface impressions," she said lightly. "Things aren't always what they seem."

"Indeed they're not."

Though his voice was soft and his expression pleasant, there was a warning in his words that she could not miss. He turned his attention to his steak, slicing into the barely seared meat to release a thick stream of rich red juices. He sensed her eyes upon him and he glanced up at her and smiled.

A shadow flickered across his face then, causing the torchlight that was reflected in his eyes to take on an almost feral gleam. Aggie quickly looked away, her pulse speeding. There was something very compelling about this man, and not a little disturbing.

Aggie reached for her wineglass. She said, "Tomorrow we'll see about getting you some of the necessities of life. Clothes should probably be first on the list. Then—"

"I want to work," he interjected. "I'm not accustomed to being idle."

She was surprised by the decisiveness in his tone. She could very well imagine this man giving an order and dozens of people scurrying to obey.

"Well, yes, of course. But first we'll have to find what you're suited for—"

"It doesn't matter," he interrupted firmly. "Whatever I'm suited for was in a lifetime long ago, and it's gone now. I have to meet the demands of today, and that means work."

There was a flinty look in his eyes, determination in the set of his mouth. Aggie had no intention of arguing with that kind of resolve.

"Well," she said. "That's that, then."

"Yes. It is."

He softened his expression as he looked at her, and Aggie wondered if he knew how fierce he had sounded.

"Of course," he added, "I'd appreciate your help in finding a job—suitable or not."

Aggie hesitated a moment, then grinned. This was not at all the way she would have approached the situation, but whose life was it, anyway?

"If you say so," she agreed with a cheerful shrug. "First thing tomorrow morning, we check the classifieds."

He gave a decisive nod of his head and turned back to his steak. "In the meantime, I'll repay your hospitality by putting your garden in order. The lawn needs trimming and the flower beds want weeding and the flagstones are loose in a few places."

"Oh, you don't have to—" She started to protest, then caught herself, abashed. "Actually," she admitted, "I have been meaning to do some yard work. It's not my favorite part of owning a house. If you want to help out, I'd appreciate it."

He nodded in acknowledgment and stabbed another slice of meat.

There was something lustful and elemental about the way in which he enjoyed his meal, the decisiveness with which he attacked each slice of meat, the pure sensuality with which he savored each bite. Watching him, she could almost taste the wine on his tongue, the unadorned flavor of rare fresh beef, unseasoned potatoes with the faint piquancy of their earthy origins... The flash of his teeth, the movement of his throat, the deft sure movements of his hands. His personal magnetism was hypnotic, and watching him was almost an erotic experience.

Aggie's face grew warm with these unexpected observations, and she hardly had any need to taste her own food. She reached for her wineglass and drank deeply, but that only increased the heat inside her veins. Michael glanced at her, lifting his glass to taste.

"Is something wrong with your meat?" he inquired. "You've barely touched it."

The sun was gone now, the twilight purple and secretive. The torches tossed gently in the breeze, creating wildly gyrating shadows around the edge of the patio and dancing lights in the lake. Michael's face was profiled in gold, strong and aristocratic, the mane of his hair threaded with starlight. It was not that Aggie had never noticed before what an incredibly good-looking man he was; it was simply that until now, it hadn't mattered. Or at least not much.

She cleared her throat and picked up her fork. "I'm not much of a meat eater. I'm never able to finish a whole steak." She took a bite of potato.

"Pity. It's exquisite." He popped the last bit of bread on his plate into his mouth. The way the light danced in his eyes gave him a mischievous look, as though he knew exactly what she had been thinking all this time...and didn't mind at all.

"It's hard to screw up an outdoor barbecue, but thanks. It's fun to cook for people who appreciate good food."

"May I refill your wineglass?"

"Oh." She hadn't noticed her glass was almost empty. "Just a little. Thank you."

He filled her glass and topped off his own. He sat back to sip his wine while Aggie finished her baked potato. The warmth of his gaze only made her heart beat faster, and the excited fluttering of her stomach all but drowned out her appetite.

His plate was completely empty. Not a scrap of potato skin, not a crust of bread remained. "Would you like to finish my steak?" she offered quickly. "I'm not going to eat it, honestly."

He glanced at his empty plate ruefully. "I seem to have made a pig of myself. I don't think I realized how hungry I was. The hospital food was nourishing, but not very good. And there never seemed to be enough of it."

"Please, take this."

"No, I couldn't—"

"Here, I insist."

With her knife and fork she lifted the steak off her plate and he slid his plate over to receive it. A grin flashed in his eyes as he leaned forward to help her.

"Food sharing," he observed. "The oldest ritual of intimacy between male and female in existence."

"I don't think that you've lost nearly as much of your memory as you might want us to believe," Aggie replied.

Michael sat back, picking up his knife and fork. "It's not just humans, either, you know. Sharing food is a fundamental way of demonstrating trust and companionship among all species."

"And not just among males and females," she pointed out.

He chewed thoughtfully for a moment. "And what is the connection between females and the nurturing instinct?"

Aggie smothered a smile behind her wineglass. "I haven't the faintest idea."

His eyes glinted at her. "You are truly lovely," he said. "And even more pleasant to be around when you're discussing something other than my social reform."

Her pulse fluttered with the unexpected compliment, and the way he smiled made her think that he knew it, and in fact had said it only to make her heart beat faster. He turned back to his steak, and Aggie didn't speak until she was sure she could make her tone casual.

"I can't be sure," she said, "but if I had to guess, I'd say reform in that area is the last thing you need. Socially, I have a feeling you're my superior in every way."

He dropped his gaze briefly. "I'm no one's superior," he said quietly.

But the shadowed mood was gone as quickly as it had come, and he glanced at her again, cutting into his steak. "Besides, didn't I hear you say recently one shouldn't draw conclusions from surface impressions?"

Aggie leaned back in her chair, cradling her wineglass, smiling. "You're a special case."

He gave that a moment's thought. "There I might agree with you. What kind of special case remains, of course, a matter for debate."

"Shall I speculate?"

He applied the knife and fork to the remaining portion of his steak with vigor. "Be my guest."

"You're well educated," she began. "Articulate, composed, confident. You carry yourself well."

He inclined his head in acknowledgment of the compliment.

"That kind of self-possession doesn't happen by ac-

cident. It's a product of environment, training...
breeding, if you will. You come from wealth and priv-
ilege. You probably went to an Ivy League school.
You're accustomed to dealing with the rich and the
powerful. If I had to guess, I'd say you are one of
them." She sipped her wine and shrugged. "You're a
society lawyer, an investment banker, maybe a corporate raider. Whatever you do, you do it well—with
style, élan and decision."

Michael regarded her silently for a time, one elbow
resting casually on the table, his finger absently tap-
ping his cheek. Even that gesture seemed, somehow,
to suggest power.

"All right," he said. "I can't tell you what college
I attended but I agree, I do seem to have some remnants of a higher education. And granted, the kind of
Manhattan real estate I keep picturing when I think of
my office doesn't come cheap."

"And they don't give windows to minor executives," Aggie pointed out. "You said there were windows."

He smiled. "You are quite the detective, aren't
you?"

She gave a modest lift of her shoulders. "I used to
be an investigative reporter, remember? I picked up a
few things."

Then he said, "So how do you imagine I managed
to get from such an exalted state to lying naked and
nameless beside a deserted road outside of Seattle,
Washington?"

Aggie sighed. "That I haven't quite figured out
yet."

He said reflectively, "We may never know."

The prospect did not seem to bother him.

Aggie sipped her wine. "Michael, did it ever occur to you that you might be married?"

She found the surprise in his eyes gratifying; she couldn't exactly say why.

"No," he replied without hesitation. "How could I forget a thing like that?"

"You've forgotten things some people might consider even more important," she reminded him gently. "Your name, age, home, occupation..."

But he was shaking his head long before she finished. "I'm not married," he said. "I'm sure of it."

She refused to be relieved by his certainty. It didn't matter to her at all one way or the other. She was sure of it. But she would have been a great deal less happy if he hadn't been so confident.

Still, she was compelled to follow logic, even if it did mean playing devil's advocate. "If not a wife, then a girlfriend. A mother, a father, brothers...a secretary, a senior vice president. Michael, you're not the kind of man to be completely alone in the world. Someone is missing you, worrying about you, looking for you. I know that as surely as I see you sitting before me now."

He was quiet for a time, staring into his wine. The light shadows that flickered across his face did not seem so playful now. When he looked up, his smile was strained, his eyes haunted.

"Do you know what I think?" he said. "I think that there are two parts to me—one that may have had an office with a window in New York, someone who ran away from something too horrible to remember. And another part who wants nothing more than a view of the lake and a job I can do with the sweat of my brow. Just like there are two parts of you," he added, and his smile gentled, became more genuine. "The part that writes sharp, cynical columns about single life in the nineties, and the part that lives in a doll-house and learns to cook gourmet dinners for someone who isn't there."

Aggie flushed and swallowed an unexpected tightness in her throat. She lifted her glass again. "And now you surprise me. I wouldn't have taken you for the sentimental type."

He leaned back in his chair, and gazed out over the lake. "How odd," he murmured. "Even I can't tell you what type I am."

He looked suddenly lonely, sitting there only a few feet away, yet completely cut off from the world he might once have known. Only moments ago, Aggie had felt intimidated, although admittedly excited, by his power, and from the beginning she had sensed danger in him. But for that moment, however brief it might be, she saw him as a tragic figure, not a threatening one.

She leaned across the table, and placed her hand lightly atop his. "Maybe," she suggested, "we can find out together."

His eyes dropped to her hand, and just as she was about to withdraw it, he turned his hand over and enclosed her fingers with his. In his other hand, he held his wineglass, and he lifted it to her in a salute. His eyes were as absorbing as moonlight on water. "To discovery," he said.

As she drank the toast, she felt enraptured by promise, caught up in possibilities she could not yet even imagine. It was a strange and magical moment. She was locked in his mesmeric gaze, like floating underwater with all the world above muted and blurred by that unique perspective. When she emerged from his spell, she almost felt as though she should gasp for air.

She withdrew her hand and glanced at her wine-glass. Empty. ''Well,'' she said brightly, pushing up from the table. ''I should get these dishes cleaned up.''

''I'll help.''

Together, they carried the few dishes into her small, brightly lit kitchen. Michael handed her the plates from the doorway while she loaded them in the dish-washer, but still his presence crowded the room.

She closed and locked the dishwasher and turned to him, wiping her hands on her skirt a little nervously. ''Well,'' she said, ''is there anything you need? Did I show you how to work the coffeemaker? Do you have plenty of towels? I brought an extra blanket. It can get chilly at night.''

He stood framed by night, magnificent and virile, and his smile was too understanding of the cause of her sudden outburst of chatter. She wondered if she should mention—casually, of course—that all the doors had dead bolts and that she kept a baseball bat under her bed. Immediately, she rejected the idea.

''Thank you, Aggie. I think you've thought of ev-erything. You've been so kind, I hesitate to ask an-other favor but...''

Even through her unreasoning trepidation, Aggie knew there was only one response. ''Don't be silly. What is it?''

He reached up and caught his hair back in one hand at the nape of his neck. ''Scissors,'' he said.

She gaped at him. ''You're going to cut your hair?''

He nodded. ''It's hot and inconvenient, and I can't

imagine why I kept it this length. Besides, it's—'' his eyes were evasive ''—distinctive.''

Aggie understood immediately. He was really worried about who might be looking for him, and his hair, by both its color and length, was one very distinguishing characteristic. Without it, he wouldn't exactly blend into the crowd, but he would certainly draw fewer stares.

She gave a decisive nod of agreement. ''Pull up a chair. I'll get the scissors and a towel. I won't promise you a salon-quality job, but it will be better than your just chopping it off at the neck.''

After collecting the proper utensils, Aggie seated him under the imitation Tiffany-shaded light fixture in the center of the kitchen and draped a towel around his shoulders. She pulled back his hair with her fingers, and she did not think she imagined the way he tilted his head a little to her touch, instinctively seeking a caress. She liked that.

She draped Michael's hair over the chair back, letting her fingers linger for just a moment on its silky texture. Then she took a deep breath and picked up the scissors. ''Okay, here we go,'' she said. ''You're sure you want to do this?''

''Positive.''

Aggie caught his hair in one hand just below his collar, and made a single decisive cut all the way across. Four inches of satin locks came away in her hand. She winced, hoping he wouldn't regret what she had just done.

''Do you want to save it?'' she inquired, showing him the souvenir.

He laughed. ''And do what? Weave it into a belt?''

She opened the trash can and dropped the hair inside. "Maybe I should save a strand or two. I did a story once about voodoo, and it seems a strand of hair is one of the primary ingredients to casting a spell."

"And what kind of spell would you cast?"

He tilted his head back as she returned to stand behind him, blue eyes teasing her, and Aggie knew exactly what kind of spell she would cast, if she had the chance. Which was of course ridiculous.

She pushed his head back into position firmly. "When I get my license to practice voodoo, I'll let you know."

Carefully, she began to shape and style his hair, using the comb and tiny snips of the scissors to trim it to a length that was just above his collar line. She leaned close as she worked, her abdomen and thighs pressed against the back of the chair, her breasts level with his eyes, had he turned his head. He did not. He didn't have to. She was aware of him on the most basic, essential level—of his shape, his scent, his strength, all of the things that composed his maleness—just as he was aware of her.

The awareness was like a low-level electric hum in the air between them, and for a long time neither of them spoke. Aggie focused on the scissors, the texture of his hair taking shape beneath her hands, the warmth of the skin of his neck, the breadth of his shoulders.

Then he said softly, "I can hear your heartbeat."

The scissors poised in midair and Aggie's heart actually gave a little jump. "You cannot."

"Yes, I can." He spoke quietly and matter-of-factly, and he didn't turn his head. "Just now, I surprised you. It stuttered a little."

Aggie made the scissors close on the little snippet of hair she had been about to trim, her throat dry.

"And now I've frightened you." Still he didn't move his head.

"Not at all." She forced lightness into her tone. "I was just thinking you're the one who must have nerves of steel—to tease a woman who's working this close to your head with scissors in her hands."

She took the comb from her pocket and swept it through his hair, then carefully folded and removed the towel from around his shoulders. She produced the hand mirror she had brought from her bathroom and stood behind him, framing his newly cut hair with her hands. "What do you think?"

He held up the mirror, but she could see his eyes were not on his own reflection. They were on her.

Aggie dropped her hands to the back of the chair. He lowered the mirror to his lap.

He said, "Aggie, I have to be honest with you. I know I told you I would make myself available for your columns, and in a sense we had a deal...but I can't promise you how long I'll stay."

"I know that," she said quickly. "That was always understood. As soon as your memory returns, or we find the connection to your past..."

He shook his head. His short hair lay neatly against his neck, and barely rippled with the movement. "Or not. I don't want you to count on me to be here. I may not be able to stay."

"I don't understand." She frowned, puzzled, and stepped away from the chair. "You're safe here. You're comfortable, aren't you? I can help you, or at least try. Where would you go?"

He sighed and shook his head again. "I don't know. I don't know the answer to any of those questions."

He half turned in the chair and lifted his hand as

though to catch hers. His hand brushed her thigh, instead, and, rather than withdrawing, he let his fingers linger there, lightly caressing the folds of her skirt.

Aggie's heart was pounding so loudly now, she would have believed he could hear it; she wouldn't have understood how anyone in the room could have heard anything else. He lifted his eyes, and watched hers. His fingers slowly curved around her thigh, just above the knee. With a gentle pressure, he drew her closer. She didn't resist. She didn't have the muscle power to resist, even if she had had the will. And she didn't have the will.

His fingers stroked the inside of her thigh, gathering and releasing the material of her skirt, holding her with nothing more than that one hand, that light embrace. His breath was hot on her abdomen, slow and steady. He said, softly, "Yes. I am safe. But are you?"

Aggie's muscles were like molten lead, thick, syrupy, heated to the boiling point. She put her hands on his shoulders to steady herself; she tried to take a deep breath, and thought, *Don't stop touching me. Don't stop...*

"I think this is a mistake," she said.

"I know it is," he agreed.

His voice went through her, rumbled through her like the low vibration of an earthquake, reverberating through nerve endings and cell fibers and causing her very essence to quiver for him. She thought, this is insane.

Aggie said, "I think it's time we said good-night."

His eyes were on fire. So was her blood, every part of her, heated and liquid.

"I think you're right."

And then, still holding her thigh in that gentle, maddening, caressing embrace, he brought his face forward, and he kissed her abdomen.

She went weak with it. Searing heat penetrated her, melted through her, tightened in her deepest, most sensitive core. His lips parted, mouth open and drawing her in, his breath dampening the thin cotton material that separated him from her flesh. She gasped out loud from the sensation of it. Her fingers tightened on his shoulders. She actually felt her head spin.

And then he released her, turning his face to rest for a moment against her stomach. Aggie spread her trembling fingers through his hair, caressing him. The sound of their breathing, unsteady and intermingled, played a symphony with the chorus of tree frogs outside the window.

Then he took both of her hands in his, holding them as he stood. Her heart began to thud again as she waited for him to speak, or to move.

But he simply took her hands and, one at a time, turned each palm upward to his lips. His kiss traveled along her nerve endings and made her spine tingle. Then he raised his eyes to her.

She stared.

His eyes. They weren't his eyes at all, they were different, they weren't like the eyes of any man she had ever seen before....

And then it was gone. She blinked, and his eyes were the eyes into which she had looked all day, alight with passion, gentled with regret. He said, ''Good night, Aggie.'' And he left her.

Aggie stood at the window and watched him walk down the path toward the office, her heart still beating hard. She had not imagined it this time. Right before her very eyes, Michael's pupils had changed shape, going from round to oval…like an animal's.

She stood at the window long after he had disappeared into the shadows, wondering if he was out there somewhere, watching her, too. She stood until the moon came up and the mist spirits began to dance on the lake, then, shivering, she turned and locked the door.

CHAPTER SEVEN

*H*eartbeats. Always, in the background, was the rhythmic beating of hearts. Michael was dreaming about the moon, faces floating in and out of the moon... Whose faces? The old man, he knew him well, and regarded him with equal measures of devotion, fear and respect. A woman in a black dress, gold hair, sleek and sophisticated. An older woman, regal, silver-haired; he adored her. Other faces less distinct, features blurred but expressions remembered: shock, question, shame, awe, wonder, a flash here and there of secret satisfaction. They were at a table, a long table in a many-windowed room, and on the wall a bronze plaque...the moon. The shadowed moon.

Heartbeats.

Running. Mist and drizzle, the smell of dampness. The pounding of his lungs, the lengthening of his muscles, speed, glorious speed. Moon shadows on night clouds, the racing of his heart, the exhilaration of the chase. Power. Thrilling yet terrifying. And then a snuffling behind him, the smell of danger, hot and wild, growling, panting, the explosion of adrenaline, turning, slashing...

Michael awoke with a gasp that felt like a choked cry tearing through his throat. He lurched upright in bed, disoriented, sweating, staring at the unfamiliar surroundings through the misty light of early morning. *Heartbeats.* His own racing now. And hers, far away...

He took a few deep breaths, calming his thundering pulse as he gradually reoriented himself. Aggie's little house. Her office with its view of the lake, the sofa that made into a bed, colorful patchwork quilts. His eyes moved slowly around the room, taking comfort in the things he saw there. The computer terminal with its silent screen. The row of colorfully jacketed books. The ginger jar lamp. The little kitchenette and coffee-maker. Soothing signs of home, cheering because they belonged to her. It was good to see these things first thing in morning.

The things he had seen in the dream, he did not want to remember.

He released another long breath, relaxing by stages, and pushed his hand through his hair. And he froze.

His hair.

He flung aside the covers and leaped out of bed, plunging across the unfamiliar room in the semidark. In the bathroom, he slapped the wall for the light switch, then whirled toward the mirror.

What he saw reflected there caused horror to drain through his muscles and shock to close up his throat. He gripped the sink and stared at the image, repulsed but helpless to turn away, for a long, long time.

"Are you *insane?*"

The voice on the other end of the telephone line squawked meaningless syllables while Aggie squinted at her bedside clock. "No," she muttered. "But who-ever you are, you must be, or else you have a damn good insurance policy. Do you know what the penalty is for calling me at this hour?"

"If you hang up, I'll only call right back."

The words reached her just as she was about to drop

the receiver into its cradle. Aggie plopped her head down onto the pillow, closed her eyes and demanded, without nearly as much rancor as she felt, "Who is this, anyway?"

"You know perfectly well who it is, and you know why I'm calling, too—"

"Russ?" She opened one eye.

"That's right, Miss Do-Gooder of the year. Do you want to answer me one question? Just one question?"

She focused again on the clock. "Do you know what time it is?"

"It's almost six o'clock, whatever that has to do with anything."

"Whatever?" Aggie sat up, sleep gone now, and scowled fiercely. "What do you mean calling me at this hour of the morning to ask me stupid questions? I was *asleep,* you idiot!"

"And I go off duty in ten minutes. As a matter of fact, I was up all night working an accident—"

Aggie began to feel a twinge of remorse.

"Where who should I happen to run into but your brother?"

"Whom," she corrected, yawning. "I think it's whom."

"*Who* told me something so crazy, I called him a liar to his face, and now I need you to back me up. You didn't take that indigent home with you, did you?"

Whatever sympathy Aggie might have had for the hardworking cop completely vanished and was replaced by a thoroughly justifiable sense of outrage at his proprietary tone.

Her own tone was as frosty as she could make it at five-fifty in the morning. "I don't know what concern it is of yours whether I bring home an 'indigent,' as you so graciously put it, or a puppy, or the Prince of Wales! Who in the world do you think you are—''

"So it's true? God help me, Aggie, I thought you were smarter than that!''

If Aggie had had a whistle, she would have blown it in his ear at full volume, slammed down the receiver, jerked the phone out of the wall and kicked it around a few times for good measure. As it was, she sputtered wordlessly for the few precious seconds it took for Russ to get the conversational edge again.

"Do you know the statistics? And that's just from people being hacked to death on the streets. Who knows what happens when they bring the crazies into their homes! You used to be such a reasonable, sensible woman. What got into you? Granted, he's a good-looking man—''

Aggie said sweetly, "Oh, do you find him attractive, Russ?''

A beat of silence. Then, "Now don't you start twisting my words—''

"The only thing I'm going to twist is your arm, straight behind your back until you turn blue in the face the next time I see you, you arrogant, pigheaded, badge-polishing jerk!''

Aggie was in fine form now, every trace of lethargy vanished, and she hammered out the declaration with the precision of a machine gunman. Even Russ knew better than to challenge her in this kind of temper.

"How *dare* you wake me up to tell me what I should or should not do, how I should or should not run my life! How dare you gossip about me to my brother, who as a doctor should have told you, by the way, that there is a great deal of difference between temporary amnesia and insanity and that being indigent doesn't necessarily make you crazy! And for your information, he is neither. I'm a great big grown-up woman, Russ, did you know that? I can take care of myself!''

"I know that," he mumbled.

But she was just hitting her stride. "I can walk and talk and drive a car and everything. I can pick out my own clothes and—guess what?—even my own friends. And the only reason I haven't already hung up on you is because I suspect David is at least half-responsible for this. And believe me, he'll be hearing from me, too. All right, two reasons," she admitted shortly. "You'd better go ahead and tell me what you called to tell me, which had better be that you've picked up something on him."

The silence went on too long to presage anything good.

"Oh, come on, Russ. You've got to have something."

"Nothing," he admitted. "I even ran him through the FBI, which took some doing, let me tell you that. So far, there's no match."

"Well, I'm sure you're just thrilled about that." She weighted her voice with sarcasm. "And if all you're looking for are criminal records, I could have told you he wouldn't have one. What about missing persons?"

"I told you, we checked."

"Well, why can't you broaden the search? Maybe he's not from Washington, maybe there's a report filed on him in New York or—"

His voice was gruff with irritability. "What do you want me to do, put his face on a milk carton? Nothing's come in. We just have to wait until it does."

"Well then, you're not very helpful at all, are you?" she replied acerbically.

"Maybe, maybe not."

He hesitated just long enough to keep her from hanging up. She didn't hang up because she could tell he was trying to make up for his earlier behavior. Russ was like that—quick to fly off the handle with some macho sexist nonsense, and just as quick to realize the error of his ways.

Aggie released an impatient breath into the receiver. He didn't push his luck.

"I may have a lead on your dog," he said.

For a moment, Aggie didn't know what he was talking about.

"Was it a big fellow, rangy, looked kind of like a German shepherd or maybe a Malamute?"

"Oh," Aggie remembered. "*That* dog. What's a Malamute?"

"It looks a little like a wolf, only with long hair."

Dogs were Russ's hobby, and it was no secret he was waiting for a position to open up on the police canine corps. He had been on a waiting list for over two years.

"I don't know," she told him. "It was hard to tell, I really didn't have much of a glimpse. Why?"

"Do you know where the Sutterville Community is?"

"Not really. What's this got to do with—"

"It's less than a mile from where you had your accident. It's pretty isolated out there, orchards and farm country, you know. But that night, we had three—count them—three reports of wolf sightings in that area, all of them around the time of your accident.

One person actually reported two wolves running together.''

Aggie's chest felt tight and she couldn't say why. Her throat was so dry, she had to swallow, twice, before she could speak. ''Um, so what does this have to do with me?''

''You said you saw a dog that night,'' he explained patiently. ''German shepherds and Malamutes look like wolves. Maybe that was your dog.''

She murmured without thinking, without even being aware that she had spoken out loud, ''They didn't seem to think so.''

''What?''

She cleared her throat, tried to focus. ''I mean, funny they should all report a wolf, not a dog.''

''Yeah.'' His tone was thoughtful, and he was silent for a moment. Then he said, ''Oh, well, it could be worse. We could be in New Orleans.''

''What's there?''

''Werewolves, babe, don't you watch the news? There's some guy down there slashing people up and calling himself the werewolf killer.''

''Oh, yeah.'' Vaguely she remembered hearing something about that, but it seemed so far away and had nothing to do with her.

''Some craziness in the world, huh?''

His point was not so subtle, but she suddenly lacked the energy to call him on it.

Then he laughed and added, ''Hey, maybe our Seattle wolves are related. Cousins, or something, what do you think?''

She made herself take an interest in the conversation. ''I think you should put it over the wire right now and stop bothering innocent citizens at this obscene hour of the morning.''

"You know it's just because I care about you."

She hesitated. "I know. But don't, okay?"

The pause was longer this time. "Right. Use your head, though, Aggie. I mean it."

She promised she would, and said goodbye.

All prospects of sleep were gone and Aggie wearily got up to make coffee. She couldn't help glancing across the way at the fog-shrouded cottage by the lake and was surprised to see the glow of a lamp from the window. Apparently, Michael was an early riser.

She slipped a short robe over her nightshirt and went out the front door to get the paper. She was not in a good mood, and it was mostly because of a niggling suspicion far at the back of her mind that Russ might be right. She *was* insane.

It wasn't just that Michael was a perfect stranger, which, as her own brother had pointed out, was bad enough. It was that from the beginning, her own instincts had warned her there was something dangerous about him, and she had been attracted by that danger rather than repelled…even as she was attracted, on levels she couldn't begin to define yet, to other things about him that were equally as instinctual.

And last night, her instincts had been correct. He had made a major pass at her and she had responded as thoughtlessly, as helplessly, as a teenager on prom night. And what had happened afterward?

Nothing had happened afterward, she assured herself firmly. Whatever it was about the pigmentation of his eyes that made them appear to keep changing shape was just that—appearance. An unusual characteristic, certainly. But there was no reason to overreact.

She had been doing enough of that lately as it was.

She returned to the house, entered the kitchen and poured herself a cup of coffee and sat down at the small kitchen table to look through the paper. She began to wonder if she had taken on more than she could handle, trying to rehabilitate and reintegrate this man into society, or even by taking responsibility for him until—or if—his memory returned. What if her experiment failed? What then would she have to write about in her column?

And worse, what would become of Michael? Of her?

She glanced again, worriedly, through the window to the little structure across the way. She had been pretty high-handed from the beginning. It was probably time she had a serious talk with her houseguest about what *he* wanted. At the same time, it wouldn't hurt to set a few ground rules covering incidents like the one last night.

The only problem was, she wasn't entirely sure what she wanted those rules to be.

She finished her coffee, put on a pair of jeans and a light cotton shirt and started down the path to the office. She had the classifieds section of the newspaper in her hand. Michael could look through it, and they could talk about what kind of work he wanted to do. Then they could talk about…other things.

There was no answer to her first knock, and she called his name softly. The light was on inside, but he might have gone back to sleep. She tried the doorknob. The door wasn't locked. She would have to speak to him about that. She had an awful lot of expensive computer equipment inside. And then she had to smother a wry smile at her own foolishness. It wasn't very logical for her to worry about unlocked doors when she'd already given her key to a stranger.

She peeked inside, not wanting to disturb him if he was, by chance, still asleep. The sofa bed was in the sofa position, the bedding neatly stacked on one arm. She called, a little more loudly, "Michael? I brought you the—"

He came from the bathroom at that moment, wearing jeans and nothing else, drying his hair with a towel. He stopped when he saw her, and the towel fell away.

Aggie's hand flew to her throat. She stared at him. "My God, Michael!" she whispered. "Your *hair!*"

A lifetime seemed to pass between that moment and the next, but in fact it was hardly a heartbeat. The newspaper in her hands fluttered to the floor. Michael veiled his eyes and his expression became guarded as he moved forward and picked up his shirt. He pulled it on and tossed his barely damp hair back, combing it out with his fingers. It fell below his shoulders. Last night, it had barely brushed his ears. She had cut it with her own hands and now it was as though it had never been touched.

He met her gaze as he buttoned his shirt and there might have been a touch of defiance in his face. "I thought about cutting it again," he said simply, "but I couldn't find any scissors."

"Right-hand drawer of the computer station," she murmured absently. As she spoke, she was moving forward, hand outstretched as though drawn by some irresistible power. She touched his hair. Soft and silky. Real.

She let her hand drop.

"How could that happen?" she demanded, just as though he might know the answer. She searched his face for some hint of a secret there. "How can anyone's hair grow six inches *overnight?*"

Michael's expression grew shuttered again and he stepped away from her probing gaze abruptly. "Why are you asking me?" he returned sharply. "Apparently, that's one of the things I chose to forget about myself."

She kept staring at him. "It's not possible. Is it?"

He went to the wet bar and poured a cup of coffee. "Do you want one?" he asked, without turning.

"Um...no. Thank you."

He turned, cradling the mug in both hands. His expression was so distant and his eyes so carefully masked that it was impossible to believe he was the same man who had charmed her so last night. But he was the same. *Exactly* the same, and that was the problem.

He said, "I've given it some thought. And although I appreciate what you've done for me more than you can know, I think it's best that I move on. Whatever answers I need can't be found here. And there's always the possibility that...well, whatever trouble I'm in will follow me here. I think it's best that I leave."

"Where will you go?"

He glanced down at his cup. "That's nothing you should have to worry about."

It struck her suddenly and she shook herself out of her spell. He was talking about leaving. She couldn't let him leave, not now—*especially* not now.

"Michael, don't be ridiculous," she said adamantly. "You're not going anywhere. There are some things...some things we have to find out, that's all, and nothing has changed. Let's just..." She took a deep breath and pressed her fingers briefly to her temples. "Let's not lose our heads here."

"Aptly put."

Michael lifted his cup, started to take a sip, then changed his mind. Without another word, he walked past her through the open door to the small outside patio.

Aggie remained inside for a moment, trying to orient herself, trying and failing to make sense of the past few moments. David would know. She should ask David. And she knew that the last thing in the world she wanted to do was ask David.

She was afraid of what he might tell her.

She went outside.

Michael stood looking out over the lake, sipping coffee. She stood beside him, saying nothing, trying not to stare at him. Trying not to even notice the way the breeze ruffled his hair over one shoulder and smoothed it back from his face. *My God,* she thought as the undeniable reality struck her anew. *My God.*

Michael murmured, "All this water. It makes me feel safe."

And Aggie replied with supreme mundanity, "We're actually on a little peninsula here, almost completely surrounded by water."

He sipped his coffee again. "I have dreams," he said, still not looking at her. "Nightmares, really. They seem to be about what happened right before I ran into the path of your car. In some of them, I'm running from something, someone—both. Actually, it seems to be men with dogs who are chasing me. And in others, I have blood on my hands. I think I may have killed someone."

Aggie didn't know why this statement did not surprise her, shock her or cause her to pull back, especially in light of…other things. It seemed, in fact, to be one of the least important things about him at this point.

Was this man a killer? She looked at him now and knew the answer was yes, he could be. He would do what he had to. She had always known that about him. And if he had killed someone and *that* was the horrible secret in his past, Aggie was sure that person had needed to die. For a cold-blooded murderer Michael was not.

She should have been shocked at the nature of her thoughts, since she had always considered herself a strongly liberal person who believed that no one deserved to die at the hands of another person. But where Michael was concerned, the truth was simply the truth. She did not think he was guilty of any such crime— for reasons of logic, not emotion—but if he was, she realized slowly, she would not feel any differently toward him.

Which only left her to wonder how, exactly, she *did* feel about him. And it was far, far too early to answer that.

She said reasonably, "They could be memories. Or they could be just dreams."

The glance he shot her was quick and surprised and, she thought, perhaps a little respectful. He had expected her to either dismiss him out of hand or to run away.

"Law enforcement officers use dogs to track fugitives, don't they?" he asked. "In my dreams, I can hear them growling and snuffling."

She shook her head. "If there had been a manhunt,

we'd know it. The police have searched their files and there's nothing on you. You have no criminal record, Michael. So maybe the men who were chasing you— the men in your dreams—do."

She had expected him to be reassured by that, but he wasn't. He barely seemed to notice. He simply gazed into the lake until its silvery flatness was reflected in his eyes, and he said, "That's not all. In the dreams…I'm someone else."

That made her frown. "I don't understand."

"I'm running, but not with these legs. I feel the wind on my face and the ground beneath my feet but it's not *me*. It's something else."

She looked at him intently. She could read nothing from his face and he kept his eyes screened from her. "What are you saying, Michael? What do you think the dreams mean?"

He was silent a long time. He took another sip of his coffee. When he spoke, his tone was matter-of-fact. "There's something wrong with me, Aggie. At best, I'm seriously disturbed. At worst…there's something wrong. The very least damage I can do is bring whoever was chasing me right to your door. I can't be responsible for that."

"I think it's too late to worry about that, Michael. If you're right and someone is looking for you, all trails will lead them to me, whether or not you're here to protect me from them."

He looked at her then with surprise in his eyes. Obviously he hadn't thought of that. Neither had Aggie until the very second she had said it, a sudden desperate burst of inspiration that would keep him here for just a few days longer…just until she could figure out what was going on. Until she could decide what to do.

She hoped it was not going to be an impulse she would regret.

"Yes, I suppose you're right," Michael said. "The damage has been done, hasn't it?"

And then she took an enormous chance. She said, "Michael, this sudden decision to leave...I don't suppose it could have anything at all to do with what happened between us last night?"

She waited, breath suspended for a half second, feeling foolish, feeling vulnerable, feeling stupid. He might not even know what she was talking about. Nothing had happened between them. A caress that she'd found highly erotic, a few murmured words, an instant of panic on her part...insignificant to him, barely worth noticing, meaning nothing.

"In part. It probably won't surprise you to know I find you attractive," he answered quietly.

Her heart soared, ridiculously.

"You've been nothing but kind, Aggie, and I don't want to take advantage of that. I acted irresponsibly last night. If I stay, I'll probably do so again. That won't be good for either of us."

"I think," Aggie said, drawing a deep breath, "that's the least of our problems."

His eyes were sober. "None of this is your problem, Aggie."

She met his gaze evenly. "Yes, it is. There are some problems we're given and some problems we choose. I chose to make this my problem. And now I can't unchoose it."

He smiled faintly. "I'm not sure there is such a word."

"I'm a writer. I can make up my own words."

His smile grew sadder, more reflective. "I don't suppose you have any words for what's happening to me now." Absently, he lifted one hand and combed through his long locks.

Aggie pressed her hands tightly together, as much to give herself the feeling of courage and resolve as to add conviction to her tone. "I know I've been selfish and foolish," she said, "and for that I apologize. I said I was going to help you, but my primary concern has always been using you to get a few columns. I'm sorry, Michael. I hope you'll forgive me."

He gave a rueful little chuckle low in his throat. "As long as you'll forgive me for using you for shelter and food and a place to hide out from my enemies."

She smiled at him, and it seemed their relationship was almost back on even footing again. She said, "Well, I've been doing everything all wrong, I see that now, even if all I wanted was to get some good columns. My plan was just to pretend life was normal while we waited for your memory to return, and I now see that's not possible."

She took another deep breath, squaring her shoulders determinedly. "We've got to try to find out who you are, Michael, where you come from and what's in your past. If you are in danger, if these dreams mean someone was chasing you and they're still looking for you, we need to know that. We need to know..." She cleared her throat and darted a look at his hair. It was still as long and lustrous as it had been ten minutes ago. "About your medical background. There have got to be things we can do to trigger your memory, and if that doesn't work, I know a thing or two about old-fashioned investigation. We can solve this, but we have to do it together. If you go off on your own, you won't have a chance—and I will have missed the most exciting thing that's happened to me in years. Let me help you, Michael.''

His smile was warm, sun-kissed, parting the fog that had hovered between them the way the growing day parted the mist on the lake. ''Am I really the most exciting thing that's happened to you in years?''

''Does that surprise you?''

His expression grew rueful. ''No, I suppose not.''

''So we're agreed?'' Aggie had learned her lesson. This time, at least, she would ask his permission. ''We start today trying to find your past?''

''Quietly,'' he agreed. ''As long as we do it quietly.''

She nodded. ''I also know how to be discreet.''

''Good,'' he murmured. He returned his gaze to the lake and once again touched his hair. ''Because I'm beginning to wonder if the question might not be who I am, but *what*.''

CHAPTER EIGHT

After a promising if mostly cloudy start, the day turned rainy and dull—typical, Noel thought, of most days in Seattle if his time here so far was any indication. It wasn't even a decent rain, the kind a man could reasonably be expected to stay out of; rather, it was a messy, misty drizzle that crept down the collar and soaked through the socks and was, in short, thoroughly miserable. Just as everything about this mission had been from the beginning.

Noel found Gavin at two o'clock in the afternoon in the hotel bar. The place was almost deserted at that hour, dim and dingy. Some mindless sports game played on the television in the background, and Gavin, lounging back in a booth with a half-empty glass of scotch in front of him, pretended to watch.

Noel slid into the booth opposite him. "Congratulations," he said. "You must have completed your assignment or you wouldn't be sitting here."

Gavin lifted his glass. "Wrong," he said. "If I had completed my assignment, I wouldn't be sitting here. I'd be on my way home." And he smiled secretly into the glass before sipping again. "To a triumphant welcome."

The scotch he was drinking was apparently not his first of the day. Noel tried to conceal his irritation. "You keep up the bang-up job you've been doing and you'll be lucky if they let you go home at all. For God's sake, Gavin, have you lost the trail completely?

Because if you have, the sooner we confess we've failed, the easier it's going to go with us. If you waste more of the *grand-père's* time and money—''

''I haven't lost the trail, damn you!'' Gavin's denial was as sharp as the strike of a snake. ''I never lose a trail!''

Noel was far too used to Gavin's outbursts to be moved by this one. He sat back patiently and said nothing, waiting for Gavin to calm down.

Gavin tossed back the remainder of his drink and set the glass down loudly on the table. ''Hey!'' he shouted. ''Does anybody work here?''

''God, you are an embarrassment,'' Noel muttered, and sank back more deeply into the shadows.

A stiff-faced young waiter appeared and took Gavin's glass.

''A double,'' Gavin barked. Then, ''Hell, as hard as it is to get service around here, make it two.''

The waiter glanced impassively at Noel. ''Something for you, sir?''

Noel looked at Gavin and said deliberately, ''Club soda.''

The waiter nodded and left, and Gavin muttered, ''There's too much damn water. I've never seen so much water in my life.''

''Of course there's water,'' Noel replied impatiently. ''Do you think Michael got to be who he is by being stupid? He knows we can't track him over water so he came to the wettest place on the continent...or at least the closest. The only more effective thing he could have done would have been to get on a cruise ship, and who's to say he didn't?''

Noel paused, amused. Wouldn't that be the final irony? Because where did most of the cruise ships out of Seattle go but to Alaska…right back where they had started. And Michael was just clever enough to think of that, to leave them stranded in this miserable wet place while he sipped champagne on a luxury liner whose next stop was the last place they would think of looking for him—home.

Noel resolved to check the manifests of departing cruise ships tomorrow.

Gavin said, "He didn't get on a ship. He's here, somewhere. I can smell him."

Noel snorted as the waiter brought their drinks. "What you smell are the fumes of your own drink."

Gavin's eyes were small and malicious as they stared at him. "And you have a better plan, I suppose? What are you going to do, file a police report?"

"It is unlikely," Noel replied dryly, "that the police would accept any report concerning the man I would be forced to describe."

"Isn't it though?" Gavin's voice was heavy with sarcasm. "So you admit I'm the best chance we have? The only chance?"

"I admit nothing," Noel said glumly, "except that if we go back without him, we'll both spend the rest of our careers cleaning toilets."

Gavin's face, already lean and sharp, seemed to narrow even more with a smug expression. "Not necessarily."

Noel took a sip of the bubbling cold water, watching Gavin. He was just drunk enough.

"What do you mean?" Noel inquired.

Gavin laughed, downing half the contents of his glass in a single swallow. "The old man said bring him back. He didn't specify in how many pieces, now, did he?"

Noel was careful not to react. His mind was busy plotting, scheming, imagining, trying to decide how best to use this information.

He said casually, lifting his glass, "You're going to kill him."

Gavin scowled into his near-empty glass. "Damn right. I almost had him the other night, too, but I slipped on the grass. It was wet." And he fixed Noel with a suddenly sharp gaze. "And don't tell me you wouldn't do the same if you had the chance."

Noel replied mildly, "He's my cousin."

But his eyes had narrowed, just fractionally, completely unavoidably, with the thought. And Gavin saw it.

"You never liked him."

Noel shrugged. "I liked him okay."

"He's in your way. Just like he's in my way." He leaned forward suddenly, resting his elbows on the table, lowering his voice confidentially. "This is our chance, and you know it as well as I do. This is as close as we'll ever get to the top. All we have to do is get rid of him and it will be our chance to rule."

Insane, Noel thought. Gavin was completely insane. But if Noel went to Sebastian with the information, he would lose status immediately; there was nothing the old man despised more than someone who could not solve his own problems, however unexpected they might be. He had already risked the respect of his elder by whining to him about Gavin earlier. No, this was something he had to deal with on his own.

But the worst part was, there was a certain method to Gavin's madness. A streak of cunning behind his ravings. Gavin himself was unpredictable, uncontrollable and hopelessly ineffective; he would never be allowed to rule, no matter who he killed. Noel, on the other hand...

He tried to push the thought out of his mind. He sat back with a shrug, brushing at an imaginary piece of lint on his sleeve. "I don't care for bloodshed," he said. "It dirties my cuffs."

"Suit yourself." Gavin reached for his second drink.

"However..." Noel paused significantly, and waited for Gavin's attention. When he had it, he went on, "If I should assist you in your...er...efforts, would I be wrong in thinking there might be a position for me high up in the administration?"

Gavin relaxed, smiling. "Of course." He tossed back another healthy portion of scotch. "I always reward service justly performed."

"Good." Noel picked up his glass again. "Then we proceed as always."

Gavin smiled. "I picked up a trace of him, by the way." He threw out the pearl as though it were table leavings. "This morning, before the rain."

Noel tried not to sound too excited. "Where?"

"On the east part of town, a medical facility. St. Vincent's. He's not there now, but he was recently."

Noel's heart was thumping hard. "Any idea where he went from there?"

Gavin shook his head, lifting his glass. "But it shouldn't be too hard to find out."

Noel nodded, already planning, calculating, feeling the adrenaline surge as he neared the end of the chase. "I'll go there tomorrow and see what I can find out."

The only thing was, he wasn't quite sure what he was going to do with the information—warn his quarry, or track him down.

Perhaps he would make up his mind about that when the time came.

Aggie didn't have to call David. He called her, late that afternoon.

"I haven't needed a baby-sitter since I was ten," she told him. "And I haven't had this much attention since then, either."

"You also haven't done anything this stupid since then. I take it you're okay."

"You take it correctly."

"Any developments?"

Aggie wondered if David, as a medical man, would consider the growth of six inches of hair overnight a development, or dreams of a possible murder something worth mentioning.

"In twenty-four hours?" she replied. "What did you expect?"

He sighed. "Almost anything."

"David, I need some advice. I think I may have taken on more than I was prepared for here."

"What? Can it be?" he said sarcastically.

Aggie ignored him. "I want to help Michael get his memory back, but I don't know where to start. Isn't there something you guys know how to do?"

"Us guys as in doctor guys?"

"Come on, David, I'm serious."

He modified his tone, but only slightly. "Well, I don't know what you want. Psychotherapy? Hypnosis?"

"Does it work?"

"Sometimes. But it's tricky stuff and can end up doing more harm than good. Personally, I'd take a softer approach. These things almost always resolve themselves with time. Sometimes it speeds the process if the patient is exposed to familiar places and things. Audiovisual stimulation works well. And of course, olfactory—the sense of smell—is the strongest memory stimulant of all.''

"Fine," Aggie said, disgruntled. "But how can anyone be exposed to familiar things if he doesn't know *what's* familiar?"

"Well, there's the problem, isn't it?" He thought about it for a moment. "You could try random association. Various pieces of music, for example, until something sounds familiar, and then trace that back... Why am I helping you? I'm against this whole project, anyway.''

"Well, rest easy. You haven't been much help." She hesitated, then plunged ahead. "There's something else. Tell me what you know about hair."

"Hair?"

"Yes. What makes it grow. Specifically, could anything make someone's hair grow several inches overnight?"

He was silent so long that she almost retracted the question and hung up. Then he said, "Oh, I get it. You're working on that novel of yours again, right?"

She relaxed. The novel to which he referred was a short-lived project that had taken approximately two weeks to get out of her system. She hadn't thought of it in years.

"Yeah, that's right."

"Well, if this is an example of the plot, no wonder you never finished it. You're on the completely wrong track, kid. Certain hormones and vitamins can increase the health of the hair and may stimulate growth somewhat, but nothing will do it overnight. What is this, science fiction?''

Aggie swallowed hard. "Kind of.''

"Sorry, but it's really bad. Try something else.''

"I guess you're right. I will. I mean, you're sure—''

"Positive.''

"What about some strange disease or genetic anomaly?''

"Not my field, but the chances are—not a chance.''

She took a deep breath, and released it a little unsteadily, trying to muffle the sound from the phone. "Well, thanks, anyway, David.''

"Listen, are you sure everything's okay out there? Is there anything you need?''

"No, thank you. Everything's fine, really.''

"Okay. I've got to get to the hospital. You'll call if you need anything?''

"I'm not going to need anything.''

"All right then. I'll check with you later.''

"Bye, David.''

Aggie hung up the phone and gazed absently out the window. A misty gray-green rain had developed, blurring the lake and softening the cottage at the end of the path. A single light spilled a yellow pool on the lawn outside the window that faced her. Michael was there, possibly reading.

That morning, she had persuaded him to accompany her to the charity thrift shop in the minimall a few miles away. Only when she explained to him that all the money from sales went to charity would he allow her to spend anything on him, and then he seemed to be amused, for a short time, by the process of choosing jeans and T-shirts, dress slacks and a sport coat. He bought a baseball cap and stuffed his hair up under it, which had made Aggie laugh. He had a wonderful, quirky sense of humor and a playful spirit that Aggie wished she could enjoy, but there was too much sadness and worry beneath the surface for either of them to maintain a cheerful atmosphere for long.

He remembered buying shirts at Bergdorf-Goodman, which only confirmed what they already knew—that he lived in New York and made a handsome salary. That narrowed it down to ten thousand men, or so.

It would be very difficult to conduct a head count of New York City executives, just to see whether or not one was missing, without breaking her promise to be discreet. She had already contacted the news department at her own paper to be on the lookout for anything that might come over the wire, which was something she should have done much earlier. She had little hope, however, that anything would turn up. If no one had reported him missing by now, it could only mean his absence was not unscheduled. There was no way of guessing how long it might be before someone started to worry. Unless she released Michael's picture and made a major news event out of his story, her chances of tracing his origins were slim indeed.

As for explaining what had happened to him over-night…she had very little hope of doing that at all.

After a certain amount of debate, and with one last glance at the glow of light from the window across the way, Aggie took down the phone book and looked up the number for the university. It took her almost fifteen minutes to get the department of zoology, and another four connections to find the proper professor. By then, she was so weary of repeating her question, she wasn't even sure the answer mattered anymore.

"Let me be sure I understand you," he said. "You want to know what kind of animal has an oval pupil? That's it? That's all?"

"Yes, that's it."

"Well, it'll take me a while to compile a list. You surely realize there are more than one."

Aggie was sorry she had ever called. It was a silly query and she wasn't sure why she even wanted to know. "It has to be something familiar," she said impatiently. "A common animal, nothing exotic."

"Do you mean like the house cat?"

She wasn't sure whether or not he was being sarcastic. "Not a house cat. The pupils aren't that narrow. They're almost like a human's only…not."

He thought for a moment, apparently intrigued. "Not like a dog's, then. Dogs have very round pupils."

"Right."

Another moment of thoughtful silence. "Well, it may be a little exotic for you, and it's certainly not something you see every day, but the first animal that comes to mind is fairly well known, anyway."

"What is it?"

He replied, "The wolf."

CHAPTER NINE

Single in Seattle
by Aggie McDonald

Have You Seen This Man?

Some of you may recall my recent brief brush with death (not my own, I'm relieved to report) and the meaning of life. Like all good adventures, this one began with a surprise and has kept me wondering ever since. And one of the things I've been wondering is what it is exactly that makes us who we are. What is the meaning of personal identity?

Look around and you'll find your life is cluttered with things designed to tell the world who you are. Are you the picture on your driver's license? Most of us devoutly hope not. Are you a statistic on a W-4, a few lines on a job description, a face at the bus stop? Ask anyone who knows you and you'll get a different reply: husband, father, mother, daughter, client, customer, friend.

Who am I? Most of us haven't asked that question since college, but we've spent an inordinate amount of effort in the meantime answering it. We are the car we drive, the title we've earned, the job we do, the position we hold. The club we belong to, the church we attend, the house we own. We are our credit limit. Aren't we?

I have before me a healthy male in his mid-thirties. He's smart and funny and knows how to choose a good wine. He likes to work with his hands and sometimes quotes the classics. Once he had an office in a Manhattan sky rise, now he mows my lawn. Who is he? He doesn't know. Perhaps in that way, he's just like the rest of us.

Let me invite you, then, to join us as we start down the road to self-discovery. It's not going to be a pleasure trip. The road is potholed and riddled with blind curves and we'll probably be forced to take a detour or two that may even lead us to nothing but a dead end. Our route may take us right back where we started, and at the end of the road, we might find we've made the trip for nothing.

But maybe, if all goes well, we'll make a friend along the way. And that friend just might be our long lost selves.

Michael handed the typed sheets back to her with a smile. "It's perfect," he said. "Don't change a word."

"What about that part about the New York sky rise?" She frowned worriedly at the pages. "Is that too revealing? Because I could change that. Maybe I should."

"Leave it," he insisted. "Tell me something." He sat on the edge of her desk, his eyes looking down at her with amusement and admiration. "Whatever made you think you needed me for inspiration? You can write about anything and make it sound enchanting."

She gave a surprised, slightly stifled laugh. "Thanks, but you've read my old columns. It should be obvious by now that I'm perfectly capable of making almost anything sound dull."

"Every writer is her own harshest critic."

"Probably."

She searched for the cover sheet for the fax from among the clutter of papers on her desk. She had made a concerted effort to keep things neater since Michael had been occupying her office, but it only took moments for her to absentmindedly destroy any sense of order she had managed to create. Michael reached across her and retrieved the sheet from atop the computer monitor.

"Thanks," she said. She turned on the fax machine and pushed speed dial. "Anyway, I'd struck out lately. I couldn't find anything I wanted to write about and what I did write about sounded hollow."

"Because you didn't believe in it," Michael observed.

She shot him a surprised glance. "I didn't know it was that obvious."

And he smiled. "Maybe only to me."

Aggie fed the pages through the machine and waited for the confirming beep. She was intensely aware of his nearness, of the way soft denim stretched across his thigh, of long slender fingers, of the sharp bones of his wrist. She could feel her pulse increase in pace, simply because he was close.

And she could feel his smile, gentle and speculative, long before she looked up to meet it.

"So, Aggie McDonald," he said. "Who are you?"

She gave a flippant smile and a shrug of her shoulders as she turned off the machine. "Depends on who you ask, I guess."

"I'm asking you."

"I think there are more important questions at hand. Like who are you?"

Play the LUCKY Carnival Wheel Game...

GET YOUR 3 GIFTS FREE !

PLAY FOR FREE ! NO PURCHASE NECESSARY !

How To Play:

1. With a coin, carefully scratch off the 3 gold areas on your Lucky Carnival Wheel. By doing so you have qualified to receive everything revealed—2 FREE books and a surprise gift—ABSOLUTELY FREE!

2. Send back this card and you'll receive 2 brand-new Silhouette Intimate Moments® novels. These books have a cover price of $4.75 each in the U.S. and $5.75 each in Canada, but they are yours ABSOLUTELY FREE.

3. There's no catch! You're under no obligation to buy anything. We charge nothing—ZERO—for your first shipment. And you don't have to make any minimum number of purchases— not even one!

4. The fact is thousands of readers enjoy receiving books by mail from the Silhouette Reader Service™. They enjoy the convenience of home delivery…they like getting the best new novels at discount prices, BEFORE they're available in stores… and they love their *Heart to Heart* subscriber newsletter featuring author news, horoscopes, recipes, book reviews and much more!

5. We hope that after receiving your free books you'll want to remain a subscriber. But the choice is yours—to continue or cancel, any time at all! So why not take us up on our invitation, with no risk of any kind. You'll be glad you did!

A surprise gift

FREE

We can't tell you what it is…but we're sure you'll like it! A

FREE GIFT!

just for playing LUCKY CARNIVAL WHEEL!

Visit us online at
www.eHarlequin.com

LUCKY Carnival Wheel

Find Out Instantly The Gifts You Get Absolutely FREE!

Scratch-off Game

Scratch off **ALL 3** Gold areas

YES!

I have scratched off the 3 Gold Areas above. Please send me the 2 FREE books and gift for which I qualify! I understand I am under no obligation to purchase any books, as explained on the back and on the opposite page.

345 SDL DNXE   245 SDL DNW7

| |
| |
FIRST NAME   LAST NAME

ADDRESS

APT.#   CITY

STATE/PROV.   ZIP/POSTAL CODE

The Silhouette Reader Service —Here's how it works:

Accepting your 2 free books and gift places you under no obligation to buy anything. You may keep the books and gift and return the shipping statement marked "cancel." If you do not cancel, about a month later we'll send you 6 additional novels and bill you just $3.99 each in the U.S., or $4.74 each in Canada, plus 25¢ shipping & handling per book and applicable taxes if any.* That's the complete price and — compared to cover prices of $4.75 each in the U.S. and $5.75 each in Canada—it's quite a bargain! You may cancel at any time, but if you choose to continue, every month we'll send you 6 more books, which you may either purchase at the discount price or return to us and cancel your subscription.

*Terms and prices subject to change without notice. Sales tax applicable in N.Y. Canadian residents will be charged applicable provincial taxes and GST.

"At the present, a man who's waiting for an answer."

She laughed. "Just like that, huh?"

He reached down and took both her hands as he stood, pulling her to her feet. "Just hit the highlights," he suggested.

Aggie tilted her head back thoughtfully, feeling the warmth of his hands encircling hers even after he had released them. "I don't know if that would do it justice. I've had a fairly fascinating life."

"Is that who we are, then?" he mused out loud. "The sum of the fascinating lives we've led? Because if that's true, I really am in trouble, having led no life whatsoever as far as I can tell."

Aggie smiled to herself and thrust her hands into the deep pockets of her ankle-length skirt as she walked to the window and looked out. The lake was rippled and silvery in the sun, like a pool of cellophane.

"Who am I?" she asked. "A thirty-four-year-old woman who never expected to get this old. Who never expected her life to turn out like this." She glanced at him and shrugged. "But then who does?"

He looked interested. "Better or worse than you expected?"

She turned to face him, leaning against the windowsill, crossing one ankle over the other as she considered the question. "A little of both, I guess. I was going to be a crusading journalist who saved the world. I was going to get the plum assignments to hot spots all over the world. I was going to live on the edge. Instead, I get a steady job doing something I love most of the time, I own my own home, I'm read by thousands of people every day. What's to complain about in that?''

''Good question.''

Again she shrugged. ''I don't know. It's just that when I started 'Single in Seattle,' I didn't expect it to be my trademark. I didn't mean to become a standard-bearer for the your-chances-are-better-of-getting-struck-by-lightning-than-of-getting-married-after-age-thirty crowd.''

''Do you want to get married?''

''Is that a proposal?'' she teased. Then she lifted her shoulders again, self-consciously. ''Just add 'alone' to the list of things I never expected to be.''

She felt compelled to explain. ''It's not the old career versus home-and-family conflict, and I don't feel as though I sacrificed anything for my career...even if that career didn't turn out *exactly* the way I expected. It's just that...I don't know...in the back of her mind, every woman keeps thinking that someday the right man will come along and there will be children, and a home, and that it will add to, not detract from, everything that she has already become. It's almost a given, a promise. And then one day, you realize you're thirty-four years old and maybe the right man isn't going to come along, after all...and you feel kind of betrayed. Because what about the rest of it? The home, the children...the promise.''

Michael nodded soberly. ''I can see why it would be difficult to write a lighthearted column about life with the single crowd under those circumstances.''

''It's just that...'' She found herself blurting out secret truths as easily, as instinctively, as she might release a long-held breath, and with as little thought. ''God, I'm thirty-four years old. I know that's not old these days, but I really, really want to have a baby. I'd make a great mother, single or married, I can afford it, I have so much to offer…it just doesn't seem fair.''

She caught her breath and looked at him anxiously. "Can I tell you something? I mean, this is just between us, right?''

"Of course.''

"I even went so far as to check out some of those sperm banks,'' she confessed. "I didn't go through with it—but that doesn't mean I won't. And you know the worst part of it is that *I* feel like a traitor—like I've betrayed all those readers who look at me and say, 'Well, she can be single and happy, I guess I can, too.' Because I'm not happy. I need more. And I feel rotten about it.''

His smile was an odd, endearing mixture of sympathy and wistfulness. "I wish I knew,'' he said, "whether or not I'd ever cared that passionately about anything, or wanted anything that badly.''

Aggie let her shoulders sag, blowing out a breath that ruffled her bangs. "Maybe you're better off not knowing.''

He crossed the room to her in a single step and caught her hand lightly, holding the fingers on a level with, but not touching, his heart. "I think,'' he said, "that none of us is just one person. The wisecracking journalist and the cookie-baking mother.'' He smiled, and so did she. "The career woman and the homemaker. The person who loves her job and the woman who wants more. The important thing is to accept all the people you are, and be true to them.''

Aggie lifted her free hand and lightly touched his cheek. Then she smiled and let her hand drop. "You probably think I'm insane. I don't usually blather along about my personal problems. You're easy to talk to.''

"Aggie,'' he said simply, "after all we've been through together, I would hope you could tell me anything you wanted to...and that I could feel free to do the same.''

She said softly, "I hope so, too.''

And then she wondered how she could be so lucky as to know this man...and how she could be so foolish as to feel so good about it.

With a determined bracing of her shoulders, she pulled her hand away and gave him a quick, bright smile. "Well. Sorry for the interruption. I'll let you get back to work.''

"Work'' was, for the time being, her way of describing the method they had devised between them for stimulating Michael's memory. From the downtown library, she had checked out dozens of CDs, books on art, architecture, travel and business, along with as many back issues of periodicals as she was allowed to take. In addition, she had picked up newspapers from almost every major city in the United States. Following David's suggestion about audiovisual stimulation, she had encouraged Michael to spend every spare moment listening to music and looking through the books and periodicals, hoping something might seem familiar to him. So far, he had recognized a Degas from a private collection, which was not as much of a breakthrough as Aggie had at first hoped it might be. None of her contacts in the art world had thus far been able to track down exactly *which* private collection it was in, and the search did not look promising. But still, it was a place to start.

Michael said, "You weren't interrupting. And stay,

if you have time. Listen to the music with me. I could use the company.''

Aggie hesitated. She wanted to stay. Feeling as warm and contented with him as she did at this moment, she would be crazy to stay.

For the past few days, she had conscientiously avoided being alone with him for any extended period, and not so much because she didn't trust him as that she didn't trust herself. As though by unspoken agreement, he hadn't pressed his companionship on her and many times had gone out of his way to appear occupied so she wouldn't feel obligated to entertain him. But he must have been lonely. Aggie knew she had been.

She said, ''Sure. I can stay for a while. If you're sure I'm not bothering you.''

''The last thing you could ever be,'' he assured her, ''is a bother.''

He turned on the portable CD player he had shut off when she'd come in. She had been as eclectic as possible in her selection; in addition to the classics and show tunes she had obtained from the library were several jazz, rock and country-western collections borrowed from friends. The current tune was by a rather raucous rock band of which she had never heard. Michael winced and lowered the volume.

''I think it's safe to say I was never a fan of heavy metal,'' he said. ''Or maybe that's what caused me to lose my memory.''

Aggie went over to the wet bar and took a soda from the refrigerator. ''Doesn't anything sound familiar?''

''Oh, yes, I recognize quite a few pieces. But nothing has triggered any specific memory.''

"Michael." She phrased her words carefully because she had worried about it a lot lately. "If you did remember something...would you tell me, even if you thought it was something I'd rather not know? Even if it was something *you* didn't want me to know?"

He sat down on the sofa and picked up the soft drink he had left on the lamp table. He didn't answer immediately, and Aggie admired him for that. She didn't want hasty promises she couldn't trust.

After a moment he said, "I think I have enough problems without complicating my life—what little of it there is—with lies and evasions. I'll be honest with you, Aggie." He looked her straight in the eye as he said it. "To the limit of my understanding, I'll tell you everything I remember, and what I think it means. Will you promise me the same? Whatever you find out, even if you think I'd be better off not knowing, you'll tell me?"

It should have been easy to promise, but it wasn't. "The man you used to be might not have anything to do with who you are now," she said.

"I know that. But I still have a right to know."

And she would never, by any conceivable stretch of the imagination, have any right to keep that information from him. Even though what she found out was sure to take him away from her, possibly out of her life forever.

Her hand tightened a little on the cold soda can. She said, "I'll tell you whatever I find out, as soon as I hear it. The only way we're ever going to be able to help each other is if we can trust each other...about this, anyway."

There was no reason to explain the qualification. He knew what she meant. Until the veil over his past was lifted completely, there would always be a boundary beyond which their relationship could not go. Trust was dependent on knowledge, however much they might wish it were different. It was as simple as that. And as complex.

He smiled his understanding, and changed the subject. "Come sit down, look at the picture books with me. Did I tell you I remembered St. Paul's Cathedral? Which means I've either been there on tour or seen it on PBS. And something else. I got a job today."

She stopped in midstep. "What? How—who—"

He laughed. "This morning, I walked down to the construction site of that house they're building on the other side of the lake. I talked to the foreman and they're taking on day labor. It's nothing complex—lifting, carrying and fetching, I believe he said. But they pay fifty dollars a day in cash if you work all day."

She stared at him in wide-eyed astonishment and admiration. "Why, Michael, I don't know what to say! That's great! And probably illegal," she added with a slight frown, but it evaporated into a grin of sheer delight as she flung herself onto the sofa beside him, bouncing a little with excitement. "But great! Do you know what your getting a job proves? It *can* be done! A person with no background, no training, no help from the system whatsoever can get a start if he just tries hard enough."

"Except that I would have starved before now without you," he reminded her. "So maybe what it takes is trying, and luck…and a helping hand now and then. Anyway, it'll be good to be doing something again. And with my first day's wages, I want to take you out to dinner."

"You'll do no such thing! You'll—" She started to say something virtuous like "save" or "buy things you need" but then she caught the warning look in his eye and smothered an embarrassed smile. "I'll be delighted to accept," she amended. "Thank you for asking me."

"That's more like it," he said.

He was wearing an oft-washed collarless cotton knit shirt, long-sleeved and loose-fitting over faded jeans. His feet were bare and his platinum-streaked hair pulled back in a queue at his nape. When he lengthened his arm over the back of the sofa and drew up one leg to rest on the cushions, she could see his muscles stretch and define themselves beneath the soft material. He looked good enough to eat.

She quickly—and casually, she hoped—turned her attention away from her appraisal of him and took a sip of her soft drink. The CD ended and another one clicked into place. The first few strains of the opening overture from *Les Misérables* drifted through the room.

Michael's hand, which rested on the back of the sofa only inches from her shoulder, moved to caress her sleeve. It was a natural gesture, as easy as breathing, meaning nothing, and everything. He smiled, and stopped the caress with a gentle squeeze. "I loved that show," he murmured reminiscently.

Every muscle in Aggie's body was instantly alert and responsive to him, and she said carefully, not wishing to break the spell, "You've seen it?"

"Uh-huh. In Paris." And the pleasured recall faded into surprise as he realized what he was remembering. "In the original French."

Aggie sat up straighter. "You speak French?"

"*Parfaitement.* Also Russian, Japanese and Dutch." The excitement in his voice grew and she could practically see the memories tumbling over themselves in his mind. He swung around and started scrambling through a stack of magazines on the coffee table. "I saw the show and I had dinner with…"

Magazines spilled onto the floor as he tore through one after another until he found the one he wanted and flipped through the pages. "This man!" he declared triumphantly and held up the magazine.

Aggie stared at the photograph he indicated. "François Mitterand? You went to the theater with the president of *France?*"

"No, no," he replied impatiently. "I went to dinner with him. Or for him. It was an enormous affair, hundreds of people. But I was there!" He turned the magazine over, his expression rapt as he gazed at the photograph. "I knew I recognized him, but I thought it was just because he was in the news. But I was there!"

Then Aggie said, stunned, "You speak *Russian?*"

He was still staring at the magazine. His excitement was almost a palpable thing. "It's coming back to me, Aggie. I *do* have a life! I'm starting to remember, just like you said I would. It's working!"

He tossed aside the magazine, laughing, and took her face between his hands. "I've got to tell you, I had my doubts, but you were right all along. Aggie, love, thank you!"

And without any warning whatsoever, he kissed her hard on the lips.

It was quick, electric, heart-stopping. It was over almost before Aggie realized it had happened, leaving her with the hot throbbing imprint of him on her mouth and a painful pulsing to her heartbeat. Instinctively, her fingers went to her lips, touching where he had touched. Her breath filtered shallowly against her fingertips.

His hands were warm and tight on her face, and there was a quickening of the light in his eyes, a softening of his expression. She could see desire there, and it inflamed desire in her own blood, and uncertainty. His thumbs caressed the corners of her mouth, his fingers threaded through her hair. He said it again, two separate words, softly. "Aggie. Love."

Her heart was thundering in her chest, closing her throat. Every part of her tightened in anticipation, wanting, afraid...wanting. His face moved toward hers, she felt his breath, inhaled his scent. She trembled inside. He kissed her tenderly, deeply, on the forehead.

"This," he said, on a long slow breath that fluttered across her face, "is insane."

His forehead rested against hers; his eyes filled her vision and became all her world. She managed to whisper, "Yes."

"And yet..." He slid his forehead across hers, turned her gently into the circle of his arm and tucked her head against his shoulder, resting his chin atop her hair. "If I had only one wish in all the world, it would be to remain like this forever."

Aggie closed her eyes and let the tremulous, glowing warmth spread through her. "Yes."

His fingers stroked her hair, shaped her scalp. His warmth embraced her. Instinctively, she closed her fingers around his and felt his instant response, and a feeling flooded her chest that frightened her. She had always known she was attracted to him. She had never imagined the real danger would be in how fond she was growing of him.

He said softly, ''Aggie, I'll never be able to tell you how much these past few days have meant to me. If I never remember the life I once had, and I know I may not, having known you will be enough.''

She wanted to wrap her arms around him and lay her head on his chest. She wanted to spread her hands over the soft, soft fabric of his shirt and feel the springy texture of the hair beneath, the heat soaking through, the muscle and bone. She wanted...far more than she was allowed to have. More than was safe. More than was sensible.

Desire unfurled itself between them steadily and inevitably. Michael felt it in the heaviness of his heartbeat, the tightening of his muscles, the heating of his veins. He knew he should resist it, there was danger in the course on which his instincts led him, but the danger compelled him and he refused to turn away.

If he kissed her, it would be like the first time he had ever kissed a woman. If he held her, he would remember no other embrace but hers. And if he lay with her...

Aggie felt the change in him and she did not turn from it. He moved against her, turning her face to his, and she let her eyes drift closed. Her pulse was racing so fast she could hardly breathe. His breath, hot and moist, moved like a caress over her face, slow and deliberate, darting close then farther away, tasting but not quite touching, driving her mad with the anticipation of his kiss.

And Michael's senses were flooded with her. The rush of her breath, the beat of her pulse, the heat of her skin and the rich damp scent of her, like a tropical

garden. His parted lips moved over her face, each
breath a new dimension of sensory input to be savored
to its fullest. Her eyes, the butterfly fringe of her
lashes, the flush of pink heat on her cheeks, her nose,
the indentation above her chin, the glistening, wine-
colored flesh just inside her parted lips.

Each breath was a surrender of reason, a loss of
control, and he could feel the beast uncoiling within
him, savage and wondrous. His hand, which had caressed the silky firm musculature of her leg from knee
to thigh, now tightened there, fingers clamping into
her flesh, and with a sudden smothered sound deep in
his throat, he pushed her head back and closed his
mouth in a powerful, drawing kiss upon the yielding
flesh of her arched neck.

She gasped out loud with the force of his passion
and he felt her weakening in surrender even as the
need within him grew stronger, more dangerous, more
out of control. An aching in his flesh, a straining in
the joints of his wrists and fingers and ankles and
flashes of something in his mind—something dark and
glorious—something he once had been, something he
must soon be again. Need pounded in his veins and
pulsed in his temple, the need for Aggie, the need to
become…a need that thrilled him, and terrified him.

Aggie felt the sharp bite of his nails on her leg, the
incredible strength of the fingers that cradled her head,
the explosion of his kiss that was like fireworks inside
her head, bubbling lava inside her veins. The sudden
flare of ardor between them was beyond anything she
had been prepared for; it was enthralling, mesmeric,
rapturous. It all but blinded her to the alarm she felt
at her own escalating passion, reason that was slipping
away. And the changes she sensed in him, a difference

that was almost physical… None of it mattered or even registered in her fog-swathed mind; nothing was real except Michael, touching her.

And abruptly, he wasn't touching her any longer. He lifted his face with a sharply drawn-in breath that was like the gasp of a drowning man. His face was flushed with desire and filmed with perspiration, his expression was stunned, and…

"Your eyes," she whispered.

Michael pushed away from her and got to his feet, turning quickly from her. His vision was blurred and it was hard to breathe; his heart was thundering, trying to break through his rib cage, and not because of Aggie or his desire for her, yet integrally related to it. He had remembered something, something urgent, something terrifying, and even as he turned from her, struggling to focus, battling to control the powerful, unnameable change that wanted to come over him, the memory was filtering away. All he could remember was the look on her face, of shock and amazement, of horror and fascination…

He held his hands against his chest because they hurt, and when he was finally able to focus his eyes enough to look down at them, he knew why. It was the nightmare again, only this time it was real. Hands that were not his own. Palms widened, fingers foreshortened and closer together, covered with fur, topped with dark long claws. Not hands. Paws.

He closed his eyes, trying to steady his breathing. He heard Aggie get up and walk toward him. He wanted to run, to hide from her. But he had promised to tell her the truth. Even if it was a truth she didn't want to know.

"Look!" he cried hoarsely. He turned on her, holding out his hands.

He saw Aggie's face, puzzled and upset. Upset...but not horrified. He looked at his hands. They were, as they had been the last time, now perfectly normal human hands.

Michael released a shaky breath and sagged against the counter.

Aggie took a quick step toward him. "Michael, are you all right?"

He gave a quick shake of his head and held up his hand to reassure her. But it was another moment before he could speak. "You must think I'm crazy," he said with effort. And then he let exhaustion drain through him as he added, "And who's to say you'd be wrong?"

He had to turn away from her then, bracing his hands against the countertop and stretching his shoulders, trying to force strength back into his muscles, reason back into his brain.

Aggie came up behind him. Lightly, she touched his back. She said softly, "You remembered something, didn't you?"

He swallowed hard, twice. Then he nodded. "But it's gone now."

"Was it..." She hesitated, then strengthened her resolve. "Was it about another woman?"

Michael turned to look at her, and the anxiety and courage in her face wrapped tenderness around his heart. He smiled, and touched her cheek. "No, love, no other woman."

Then he dropped his hand, and drew a bracing breath. "When I was in the hospital, I had a hallucination. I woke up one afternoon from a nap, and my hand...wasn't my hand. It was like an animal hand, a paw. Then the image went away. I thought I was dreaming.''

He watched her carefully. "It happened again, just now. Only now, I don't think it was a hallucination. My hands...they changed. And it was more than that. It was something inside me...my whole body..." He struggled to find the words, then gave up with a frustrated shake of his head. "I can't explain. But I saw it. I can't believe you didn't, too."

Aggie was frowning, but it was a thoughtful look, not judgmental or derisive. "You hands are perfectly normal," she pointed out.

And he answered, "Now." He cast about for some way to explain to her, running an agitated hand through his hair. "It's as though...it only happens when I'm off guard, tired or hurt or distracted. It's almost like...returning to a natural state at those times, when I don't have the energy to fight it."

And then he stopped, staring at her, realizing how very bizarre what he had said sounded.

But she did not appear shocked. Her expression remained troubled, but thoughtful. She said, "Michael, just now—" she gestured behind her to indicate the sofa and what had just transpired there "—your eyes changed. The pupils became oval, and that wasn't the first time. It's...it's like nothing I've ever seen before. I was wondering—please don't take this the wrong way..." She hesitated for a moment, seeming uncertain, then plunged on. "Is it possible, could you have taken some kind of drug, voluntarily or otherwise, that would be giving you flashbacks now?"

"Do you mean a hallucinogen?"

She nodded.

He wanted to believe it. As horrible as it would be to think his mind had been tampered with, or that he had such weakness of character he might do such a thing to himself, believing that he was the victim of psychotropic chemicals was far, far preferable to believing that what he had seen was real.

And so he answered, "Anything is possible, I suppose."

But he had promised to tell her the truth. He added heavily, "But I don't think so. I think the answer is more twisted than that. I think..." His voice trailed off, and he looked down at his hands, stretching them out before him with a kind of dread fascination. "What if I *am* a monster?" he demanded softly.

Aggie came to him, covered both of his hands with hers, and said firmly, "You are not a monster."

She brought his hands close to her chest, holding them tightly. Her gaze was steady and unafraid. "Michael, listen to me," she said. "I know it might not be obvious at first glance, but I've been around the block a time or two. You can't be in the newspaper business for fifteen years without seeing just about all there is to see, or at least hearing about it. I promise you, there's nothing in your past that will shock or dismay me. Whatever you're repressing, don't be afraid of it for my sake. I'm the least of your worries."

His smile was faint and unconvincing. "Brave words. I hope you don't live to regret them."

"I know myself pretty well," she assured him. "More important, I know you, or at least the essential things about you. You're honest. You're fair. You're courageous. You're honorable. Those are some fairly major qualities, and they're not all that easy to find. It would take a lot to make them seem unimportant."

He took their entwined hands and lifted them to her face, pressing his knuckles briefly against her cheek. "You are very special," he said.

Aggie dropped her eyes, suddenly flustered and unsure. His touch, nothing more than his touch, could do that to her. This was all moving far too fast and she knew she should be afraid, but she couldn't be.

She could, however, try to be careful.

She started to move away and then she caught the glint of the gold chain around his neck. Impulsively, she reached for it, and pulled out the medallion from inside his shirt. The metal was warm with the heat of his skin, almost alive.

"Michael," she said slowly, staring at it. "Do you suppose this could be part of a crest or insignia?"

"Do you mean as in a family crest? Royalty?" He seemed amused.

"Maybe." She examined the sphere with its curious shading thoughtfully. "But other groups besides royal families have crests. Clubs, organizations, even corporations sometimes. This has *got* to mean something."

He looked doubtful. "Perhaps. But I don't know how you would ever find out what."

"Let me put the research staff at the paper on it," she suggested. "I don't know how, either, but there's got to be a way to track these things down."

He nodded his acquiescence, and Aggie became suddenly aware of their closeness, of the brush of his bare chest against the back of her hand, of the metal hexagon in her palm that held his heat, of his breath and the muscles of his throat, and how easy it would be to lift her face again and feel his mouth on hers.

She shifted her eyes, knowing he could read her

thoughts. She dropped the medallion and cleared her throat. "I should probably go."

He seemed to understand. He let her move away. "Dinner tomorrow?"

She nodded and smiled. It was good to talk about mundanities. "Will you eat seafood?" she asked.

"It's not my favorite."

She grimaced. "I know. Rare beef is your favorite."

"Lamb," he corrected, grinning. "My favorite is lamb."

"How about a little all-American café I know? Simple atmosphere, good food."

"Sounds great." He hesitated only slightly. "We don't have to go into Seattle, do we?"

"Actually, no. Is there a reason you'd rather not?"

Again he hesitated, and he looked as though he wasn't sure of the answer. Finally, he shrugged. "No. I suppose not."

It was easy for Aggie to see that wasn't the whole truth, but neither was Michael lying. He simply didn't know the truth. And that broke her heart.

She paused at the door, and gave him another reassuring smile. "Try not to worry, Michael. We'll work this out, together."

CHAPTER TEN

Michael worked from just after sunup until late afternoon, until his clothes were sweat-soaked and his muscles ached. He felt strong and capable and sunburnished, alive for the first time in—he couldn't say how long. Perhaps for the first time in his life.

That his hands were not used to physical labor was evident in the stinging blisters the day had earned him, but he didn't mind. Tomorrow he would wear gloves, and in the meantime, he would consider the blisters badges of honor. He was in good physical condition; his muscles were strong and his stamina intact, and that was good to know. He had accomplished something. He had done a job. The fold of cash he received at the end of the day was the least important reward for his efforts.

That evening, he and Aggie went to a little diner that was brightly lit and not very crowded in the middle of the week; the mingled aromas of fried foods, roasting meat and baking bread were intoxicating. People looked at them when they came in, but they were friendly glances, not hostile stares. And Aggie looked so lovely, she would draw attention wherever she went.

If he could have custom-ordered a day and ended it with the perfect evening, he could not have improved upon this one.

Afterward, they walked upon the lakeshore, with the clear starlight and a bright half moon to light their way. Michael was glad to know she didn't want to say good-night any more than he did. He put his arm around her waist. She fit naturally against him.

The only times he ever wished to have his memory back were at moments like these, so that he could offer something, no matter how small, in return for all she gave him.

"Would it be too banal of me," he mused out loud, "to observe that sometimes things happen for a purpose, and that life's darkest moments have a way of turning into something precious, even when it seems as though there's no possible way they can?"

Aggie smiled and rested her head against his shoulder. "Banal, yes. But often true, nonetheless."

He stopped walking and turned her toward him, looping both arms around her waist, holding her lightly. "Whatever I ran away from," he told her simply, "this is what I was running toward."

He wanted to say more. He wanted to say seductive, romantic things to her, to charm her, to delight her, to make her want him as much as he wanted her and had wanted her almost from the beginning. But such words carried with them a promise, implied or hoped for, and promises were the one thing he had no right to make.

But as she waited with her face slightly upturned to his and expectation in her eyes, it was very hard to remember that. He lowered his eyes and dropped his hands from her waist and turned to walk with her again.

"I had a really nice time tonight. You're a fun date," she said.

That made him laugh. "Thanks. So are you."

"I'm glad you think so, because I have a favor to ask."

"You know that's all you have to do—ask."

She slanted a glance at him from beneath a veil of lashes. The moonlight bathed her face in creamy light and turned her hair to mahogany; she looked like something fashioned from passion and imagination, almost too perfect to touch.

"You're probably going to hate it," she warned. "On the other hand, it might be just your kind of thing. It's hard to tell with you sometimes."

And then she went on in a rush, "I've been invited to a gallery opening next week. It's really kind of obligatory that I attend, I'll be representing the paper. I need an escort. Would you go with me?"

He smiled. "I'd be honored."

"It's black-tie."

A flash of memory...a tux laid out on a four-poster bed, shirt studs like polished marble in his hands, the smell of crisp linen and shoe polish...

He brought his focus back to her, and smiled again. "I think I can manage. What kind of gallery is it?"

"Do you know, I didn't even ask. I get so tired of these things sometimes—"

She gave a sudden cry and flung her arm out for balance as a corner of the gentle slope on which they were walking gave way beneath her feet. Michael caught her waist and pulled her back against him, safe from the lake edge.

She was laughing. "Well, there goes one sixty-dollar pair of sandals. Great for dancing, rotten for walking in the moonlight."

Her heart was beating against the palm of his hand, pulsing with joy and life. Her body was supple and relaxed against him, her hands atop his arm, her hair tickling his chin. Her warmth flowed over him from

chest to thigh, seeping into his skin. She smelled of
youth and laughter and sweet pears. He wanted to
draw her in like fresh air, drink her down like rich
wine.

He dipped his head and planted a gentle lingering
kiss on the back of her neck. Her breath caught in
surprise, but she sank back against him, melting into
his caress. She lifted her hand to stroke his face. Without seeming to move at all, as naturally as waking in
the morning or sleeping at night, his hand slid upward
and over her breast, filling his palm with softness and
warmth and utter femininity.

He felt her breath, low and deep and long, rush
through her lungs. He tasted the skin of her neck on
his tongue. Her fingers pressed into his scalp, holding
him, urging him. He took the lobe of her ear between
his teeth, moving his other hand to the gentle convex-
ity of her belly, pressing and massaging the flesh
through the light cotton material of her skirt. Her low
moan of pleasure went through him like a small earthquake, reverberating through his bones, turning his
blood to lava. He pulled her more tightly against him,
pressing his teeth against the ligament between her
neck and shoulder.

She whispered his name. He felt her trembling, and
his own. He heard her blood rushing through her veins,
pulsing, pulsing, fast and loud, her breath like the sigh
of the wind in the High Sierras. The night whirled
around them, stars and water, the burning light of
moonglow. Desire unfurled within him, hardening his
loins, strengthening his muscles, filling him with
power and need. He wanted to be her lover. That was
all he knew. It was plain and primitive and simple and
right, this wanting, this singular and all-encompassing

need. And he could feel her need in return, smell the musk of her, hear it in the rush of her pulse, taste it in the salt of her skin. He was inflamed.

What had started as a low and lovely blossom of desire unfurling inside his belly began to stretch and grow, to darken and expand, greedily lapping up reason and restraint. He could feel it, the beast awakening in him, and he welcomed it with a thrill, even as he recoiled from it in horror. Suddenly, he was a mass of conflicting, powerful sensations, all of them right, all of them familiar, none of them sane.

Deep within Aggie there was a thread of wonder at the power this man had over her, his almost supernatural ability to enthrall, as though some magical ether emanated from his pores to which only she was susceptible. It was a sensation she acknowledged and knew she should fight—the loss of control, the surrender to desire—but instead, she welcomed it. There was a wildness in him that touched something savage in her, a mastery and a ferocity that excited the most primitive responses in her. Through the swirling haze of her desire, she could almost feel him changing as she changed, becoming one with the passion they created between them. His arm beneath her clutching fingers seemed tighter, stronger, leaner. She felt the bite of nails on her skin where once there had been none, teeth that were sharper, muscles that were stronger... It was frightening and thrilling and she couldn't have stopped it if she had wanted to.

Michael tried to breathe deeply, grappling for control, but there was fire in his brain, a tightness of his skin. The softness of her flesh beneath his hands, the scent of her...oh, God, the scent of her. He was on fire. The moon was in his eyes, blinding him, and he

ached in every joint and muscle, as though he had
grown too large for his skin, as though something inside him were straining to break free and that terrified
him. His heartbeat, her heartbeat, roaring in his ears.
The heat of the moon on his face. Something was happening to him…something…

His hands pressed into her flesh, gathering her close,
even as a far and distant voice warned, *Let her go,
don't do this, she isn't yours, back away!* in a rush of
thoughts he barely recognized as words, hardly knew
as language. His nails were longer, he could feel them
growing, his feet lengthening inside his shoes, leg
muscles tightening—*insanity, insanity*—and his hands,
oh, God, his hands, he could feel them and soon she
would, too…

With a ragged gasp, he pushed himself away from
her and took a staggering step into the shadows. It was
like breaking the polar lock between two magnets; in-
ertial force made him stumble. That and his feet,
which weren't his feet at all, and his back, which hurt
so badly, it was hard for him to stand upright.

Aggie whirled, her skirts floating gracefully around
her. Her face was moon-white, her eyes enormous, but
there was something different about her, something
fuzzier and less defined. It took him a moment to realize he was seeing her through different eyes.

"Michael?" There was alarm in her voice. The residue of passion still wafted around her like a rich perfume.

She took a step toward him and he flung out an arm,
backing away.

"No!" His voice was hoarse. It was so hard to talk,
to form the words. "No, don't… Please, I'm sorry.
Don't."

"Michael, what's wrong?"

She was frightened now. So was he.

"I can't..." His breathing was labored, he tried to disguise it. Terror ran through him like a series of hot and cold chills. He couldn't let her see him. He had to get away from her, from her scent, her voice, her heat. "Aggie, please, just go to the house." Tremendous effort. "Leave me alone. I can't talk to you now."

"I can't leave you like this!" She was hurt, worried. "What did I do? What's wrong?"

"Aggie, please!"

A shout, a roar. It startled her, and made her step backward.

He whispered, "I can't... I'm sorry."

And he did not wait for her to reply. He turned and pushed through the shadows, away from her, away from his cottage, into the wilderness of the lakeshore.

Aggie called out again and took a few running steps to follow him, then stood still, seized by a primitive superstitious fear. For out of the darkness, gleaming at her from the direction in which Michael had gone, she caught a glimpse of phosphorescent animal eyes.

With her heart pounding in her ears, she turned and stumbled back to the house, locking all the doors and checking them twice. And though she sat by the window for hours, peering through the curtain for Michael's return, she never saw him.

Along the way, he left his shoes. At some point, he tore off his shirt. Then he was running and he wanted to run forever, he wanted to strip off his clothes and let it happen, this thing that was embracing him in its grip, this beautiful and terrifying and perfectly *right* thing; he wanted to let go of his reason and give in to the madness. He would have except for the voice, except for Aggie. Because that was what the voice said, nothing but her name, over and over again, and there was plaintiveness and longing in the word. Because Aggie wasn't his. And never would be.

He stripped off the last of his garments in the dark and waded chest-high into the lake. Then he began to swim, letting the water cleanse him and protect him and make him whole again.

He swam until he was exhausted, and when he climbed out and collapsed on the grassy bank, the moon had set. He looked across the lake in the direction of her house, and it was dark. He was glad.

Not once during the entire time had he looked at his own body. Now, in the cover of darkness and with nothing but his normal night vision, he sat up and slowly examined his feet, his legs, his hands. They were all normal, male and human. Just as he had known they would be.

He gathered his clothing and dressed. Then he walked back to the cottage and fell into a drained and enervated sleep.

He was dreaming and he knew he was dreaming. It was the chase again, but the blurred edges had disappeared from the dream; the images were sharp and clear. He was running and he was strong, the wind was in his hair and filling his lungs. He could hear the crackle of every leaf, the tumble of every pebble his passage disturbed. And he could hear the sound of those behind him, swift and sure, powerful chests expanding, muscular forelegs pulling, scattering earth, gaining ground. Wolves, sleek and strong. They weren't dogs at all. They were wolves.

The knowledge excited him, infuriated him, terrified him. They were close but he was faster. Faster, surer, stronger. He would run if he could; kill if he had to. And when he felt something snag his shoulder, his instincts were as sharp as fangs. He spun with claws slashing, teeth tearing; he ripped at flesh and tasted blood and the high thin whistle of exhilaration filled his ears. His teeth ripped again, and the coppery sweet warmth filled his mouth and far in the background was the screaming but he didn't care, didn't hear it, for he tore again while the creature in his grip thrashed and writhed.

"Michael! Michael, for God's sake!"

Words...

"Michael! Please!"

The screaming wasn't in his head. It wasn't...

"*Michael!*"

The dream dissolved into a thousand broken fragments around him. He was in a room, not his own room—*oh, God, Aggie's room!*—and she was pressed back against the headboard, her hair tousled and her face chalk-white, the bedclothes tangled around her, her eyes terrified and staring. He wasn't dreaming. The screams had been real.

He gasped, "Aggie!" and reached out a hand as though to reassure her.

She gave a cry and shrank farther away from him, and then he saw what she saw and his heart stopped beating.

His hands were covered with blood.

Aggie scrambled out of bed as he stumbled backward against the wall, and in a moment of utter terror and disorientation, she didn't know whether to run to him or to run for help. It had happened so fast. She was sleeping, she had heard a sound, and by the time she had dragged herself out of sleep, he was standing over her, and the gleam of his eyes and the sound of his breathing and the blood on his hands filled her with terror.

In the bluish light of dawn, his face was moon-white, his breathing was ragged and gasping, his hor-rified gaze fixed on his hands. He was wearing the baggy cotton sweatpants in which he presumably slept, and his face and hair were drenched with sweat. The flesh of his arms and shoulders seemed to be prickled with cold. The blood was coming from a jagged cut on his right forearm and smeared everything he touched—his hands, his chest, the wall—with a thin red film.

Aggie bolted to the adjoining bathroom, flipping on light switches as she went, and returned in only a sec-ond with a handful of towels. Michael was sitting on the floor, his shoulders braced against the wall, head back, eyes closed, drawing in deep shaky breaths that alarmed Aggie.

"Oh, Michael." She dropped to her knees beside him and reached for his injured arm. "What have you done to yourself?"

His eyes flew open and his fingers clamped around her arm, hard enough to make her wince. "Aggie!" Eyes that were dark and wild with desperation searched her face and skimmed her body. "Are you all right? Did I hurt you?"

Gently, she pried his fingers loose. Even though her heart was pounding and her stomach was in knots,

concern for him overrode all other anxieties and gave
her an almost superhuman calm. "Michael," she said,
holding his gaze. "You're the one who's hurt. Let go
of me so that I can see how badly."

It took a moment for her words to penetrate. Then
he dropped his eyes to the cut on his arm and he
stared, almost in disbelief. By measures, his muscles
relaxed and he released a single long low breath as he
sagged against the wall.

"You must have been sleepwalking," she said unsteadily, carefully cleaning the area around the wound.
To her relief, it wasn't nearly as bad as it looked: the
cut was long but narrow and not very deep, and the
bleeding had slowed to a mere ooze.

"I was dreaming," he said, his face turned away
from her. "Another nightmare."

Aggie noticed then the glass that was scattered on
her burgundy carpet, and the broken pane in the
French door just above the lock. The door was open.
Michael must have simply put his hand through the
glass and opened the door.

She felt a little chill.

She said, "I don't think you're going to need
stitches. How are your feet?"

He looked at her blankly. "What?"

"You're in your bare feet," she said. "There's
glass all over the carpet."

He looked at the open door, the broken pane of
glass. "Oh, my God," he said.

He looked at her, his face stricken and his eyes ag-
onized. "Aggie, I..." He closed his eyes briefly and
gave a shake of his head, then looked at her again. "I
think I thought you were in danger," he said quietly,

and with heartbreaking simplicity. "Maybe the only danger you've ever been in was from me."

She examined his feet and finished cleaning and bandaging his arm, and he allowed her to do so with a curious passivity. Only when she insisted that he come into the kitchen, away from the scene of violence and confusion, and they sat in the cheerful coziness of her tiny table with the smell of brewing coffee filling the air did some of the color begin to return to his face.

He said quietly, "Now I don't suppose you'll be insisting I stay."

She filled two sunflower-painted mugs with coffee and set one in front of him. She didn't answer. She didn't know what to say. Now that the crisis had passed, it was all she could do to keep her hands from shaking so badly they spilled the coffee.

She sat down next to him. The table was so small that their shoulders brushed. She had found an old sweatshirt of David's and made him put it on because he was shivering, but his hair was still damp at the ends and he folded his hands around the steaming cup of coffee as though warming them.

She said as steadily as she could, "Tell me what happened."

"I don't know." He fixed his gaze on the coffee cup. "It was the dream. I've told you about it. Only this time, it seemed clearer. Wolves were chasing me. I attacked one of them." His voice was flat, unemotional. "In the dream, I wasn't a man. I was some kind of beast. I heard screaming—your voice, I guess—and then I was standing over your bed. The first thing I thought was—" He drew in a sharp breath and let it out. "That I had hurt you."

Aggie reached out her hand and covered his. "Michael," she said gently, "you are not a beast."

He looked at her. His eyes were haunted, and filled with such pain that Aggie's own chest tightened in response to it.

"I promised to be honest with you," he said slowly. "I wish I had never made that promise." He looked away. "Earlier last night...what happened between us..."

Aggie stopped him with a reassuring squeeze of his hand, mistaking his reticence for embarrassment. "You don't have to explain. I thought about it, and it's my fault. I pressured you, and I never should have...what I'm saying is, impotence is not such an unusual problem, particularly after a head injury, and—"

His stare was at first surprised, then vaguely amused, then sad. One corner of his lips turned down dryly in a fleeting smile. "That," he said, "was not the problem. I almost wish it was."

Something made her remove her hand from his. She had lain awake half the night, tossing and turning, trying to understand what she could possibly have done to evoke such a reaction from Michael at the height of what she could only assume had been their mutual passion. The explanation she had finally come up with was not entirely satisfactory, but it was as close as she could get. Now she wasn't sure she wanted to hear the real reason for his bizarre behavior.

He pushed up suddenly from the table and went to the back door, pushing aside the curtain that shielded the oval window there. Dawn lay over the lawn in misty gray pools; spirits danced on the lake.

He turned, and faced her. It seemed to require enormous courage for him to do so. "There's something wrong with me. I think it's the same thing that caused my hair to grow overnight. Some kind of mutation, or anomaly."

The muscles in Aggie's body began to tense, one by one, drawing in on themselves. She didn't want to hear the rest. But she couldn't *not* hear it.

He went on, "I told you before about the... hallucinations. With my hands. I was never sure they were hallucinations. Now I am."

He drew in a breath. "Tonight when I was with you, it happened again. Only this time, it was worse, and it wasn't just my hand. It was like I was becoming someone else from the inside out. First *I* changed, then my body started to change. Literally. I could feel it. It terrified me, and I didn't want you to see me...that's why I acted the way I did."

Aggie could feel her heart pattering against her rib cage like raindrops on a tin roof. It was only by sheer force of will that she made herself hold Michael's gaze. She kept thinking about X rays, blood tests... David's voice: *They say it's not even human, for God's sake!* And what if it hadn't been a mix-up at the lab? His eyes...

Impossible. Crazy.

She said, in an almost reasonable tone of voice, "Michael, I was there. I was very, very close. If anything like that had happened, if you had...changed, I would have noticed. Wouldn't I?"

He didn't blink. He simply looked at her, sadly and tiredly. "Didn't you?" he said.

She stared at him. She swallowed hard. And she had to look away.

Crazy...

But hadn't she? Had it been real? The bite of nails on her flesh that seemed sharper and longer than Michael's had been, the increased heat of his body—the *flame* of his body—all of it powerfully erotic, almost druggingly so. Her back had been against him and she had never seen his face. She had touched only his hair, the back of his neck, his arm. But she remembered the press of his teeth on her shoulder, almost painfully sharp at one point, and the lean strength of his muscles beneath his shirtsleeve. Stronger than she remembered? The snare of eroticism in which he had entrapped her had been paralyzing, all-encompassing, self-perpetuating…nothing he could have done at that point would have frightened or shocked her as long as it did not disturb the web of pleasure he spun.

It was always like that with him. She willingly submitted to the hypnotic power of desire, so that she wouldn't notice, couldn't notice…

He said in a curiously flat, matter-of-fact tone, "Maybe that's how it all started. Maybe that's why they were chasing me in the first place—because I'm a freak."

She was crazy for even considering it. But there was the incident with his hair. That was indisputable. And tonight, something had happened…something.

And what *about* the blood tests? What about joints that showed evidence of repeated dislocation. What about…

But when she raised her eyes to him, almost dreading what she would see, she was immediately flooded with shame for her doubts. Because what she saw was a man tormented by nightmares and his own self-doubt, hollow-eyed, rumpled, slumped with fatigue. His first concern had been for her. Even as he stood in an unfamiliar room bleeding from a wound he could not remember having incurred, his first thoughts had been for her safety. Should she be afraid of him? Probably. He had broken into her house, he had exhibited extremely bizarre behavior and now he was displaying symptoms of a delusional personality. But she wasn't afraid.

"Michael, would you see a psychiatrist if I arranged it?"

He didn't seem insulted or surprised by her suggestion. He merely shook his head tiredly and pushed his fingers through his hair. "I know you mean well. But I need more help than a psychiatrist can offer, and I'm afraid of what will happen if I stay here."

"I'm not."

He stared at her.

"I'm not afraid," she said. Her hands tightened on the coffee mug with a sudden determination, and she knew it was true. "If you were going to hurt me, you could have done so tonight. You could have done it any time since you've been here, as a matter of fact, but you haven't. I don't think you're capable of it."

"You have no reason to trust me."

"But I do. And now I'm asking you to trust me. Maybe you're right. Maybe there's something genetically off kilter with you. If so, we can probably find out. But maybe it's simpler. I want you to have a psychiatric evaluation, Michael. And I don't want you to do anything drastic until you get the results. Will you do that for me?"

His face softened as he looked at her, and puzzlement shadowed his eyes. "After tonight, after what I've just told you, when even you admit I need psychiatric help, why would you want me to stay?"

She tried to make light of it with a shrug. "I really need a date for that gallery opening."

He didn't smile.

She said, "I'm not sure I'm ready to answer that. But I have a stake in what happens to you. And you owe me the chance to see it through."

Once again, he pushed at his long hair, and he released a sighing breath. He looked at her with the equal moisture of reluctance, resignation and tenderness in his eyes. "All right," he said. "Make the appointment. I'll have an evaluation."

And then he smiled, although it seemed hollow. "And buy a new dress for the opening. If you still want me, you've got a date."

CHAPTER ELEVEN

Castle St. Clare, Alaska

Sebastian stood at the tall window and admired the glint of late-afternoon sunlight on the glacier lake below. As clear as glass, as bright as a mirror, it reflected every detail of the thick blue spruce and snowcapped mountains that surrounded it. All his life, Sebastian had taken comfort from that lake, the peacefulness, the sheer inarguable beauty. He had had the balcony built off his private suite simply so that he could sit outside and gaze at the lake. But the early September air was chilly, and he now preferred his pleasures by the comfort of the fire. He was getting old.

He heard the soft pad of footsteps behind him and turned as Clarice entered the room. She was a magnificent wolf, tall and graceful with a sleek silver coat that age had not dulled. She came over to him and stood close; he dropped his hand onto her head. He could not remember a crisis in his life during which Clarice had not sensed his need, and come to comfort.

"Ah, Clarice," he murmured softly, stroking her ear. "You always know, don't you?"

She nuzzled his knee in agreement.

Sebastian hadn't heard from Noel in weeks. Not, of course, that he expected daily updates. He was not the kind of man who required constant reassurance, and his lieutenants knew better than to bother him if they had nothing to report.

Nothing to report. That was his son out there, his favorite heir. The entire future of their race rested on Michael's shoulders. How could this have gotten so out of hand?

He went over to the curved sofa drawn up before the fire and sat down, reaching for the glass of wine he had left there. Clarice climbed up and sat beside him, gently nudging her head under his arm. He smiled and slipped his arm around her shoulders; she stretched out with her head on his lap.

"Was it too much pressure?" he wondered out loud. "Did we ask too much of him too soon?"

But even before he formed the words, he knew the answer. Michael was strong, determined, ultimately capable. There wasn't a thread of weakness in him, and he knew exactly what he wanted. The problem was, as Sebastian knew very well, that what Michael wanted and what Sebastian wanted for him were two entirely different things.

He couldn't begin to fathom what Michael thought he could accomplish by disappearing the way he had, and he wouldn't know that until Michael himself told him. He did know that what had begun as a dramatic gesture had now escalated into something far, far more serious. Michael had stayed away too long. He had deliberately eluded detection. He had made himself vulnerable, and his fate was now in the hands of Noel and Gavin.

Noel and Gavin. His hand tightened a little in Clarice's fur as he realized he might well spend his remaining years preparing one of them, instead of his own Michael, to take his place. Gavin was out of the question, of course. But Noel…Noel had potential. He was close to the direct line of descent. He was bright, perhaps brighter than anyone had ever noticed before. His business acumen was as sharp as any Sebastian had ever seen and no one would deny his division was the fastest-growing in the corporation. He was a perfectly logical choice for second-in-command and no one would have been surprised had Michael named him so when he took over.

But was Noel a leader? Could he be trusted with the dynasty they had built, the moral, financial and personal welfare of all their people?

Or perhaps the real question Sebastian should be asking at this point was could Michael?

Sebastian had lived more than his share of years and it had been a full rich life. But he hated getting old. Especially when there was so much he had to attend to, so many crises that demanded his attention.

There was that renegade in the South, that mentally unbalanced throwback to an earlier time that was an embarrassment and a horror to them all. There were business complications and crises that grew more threatening by the day, and whispers of serious unrest in the Montreal office that could have repercussions throughout the company. Now rumors were beginning to filter down from the family historians about lost branches of the family, others of their kind hidden in remote places and living their own remote lives. How long before someone took those speculations seriously and started to investigate?

There were secrets Sebastian had yet to share, catastrophes he had yet to avert, destinies that were still his to arrange. He had counted on having more time.

He had counted on having help.

"Michael," he whispered into the fire. "Come home. Just please...come home."

Clarice looked up at him with dark liquid eyes, and licked his hand. But that was all the comfort she had to offer.

"Just don't ask any questions, please," Aggie said. "I need a referral to a good psychiatrist."

The silence on the other end of the telephone was leaden, and in its wake, visions of the battle David was fighting with himself were explicit. At length, he said, "Craig Morrison is a good man. He's usually booked up, but if you tell him I sent you, he'll probably free up some time. We play poker together sometimes."

Inwardly, Aggie groaned. The last thing she needed was one of David's poker-playing buddies. But on the other hand, there *was* such a thing as doctor-patient confidentiality, and she really didn't have much choice. She asked for his number.

"Thanks, David," she said as she copied it down. "This is above and beyond the call, I know."

"Nothing you want to tell me about, I guess."

"You guess right."

Another silence, long and awkward. She said, purely to break it, "Why don't you come to dinner sometime next week?"

"I've been waiting for you to ask. Will Mystery Man be there?"

"Probably. He got a job, you know."

"I didn't know." He sounded interested. "Good for him."

"It's just day labor, but he got it on his own."

"I'm glad for him. Really. No break in the amnesia, I take it?''

"A little.'' And she sighed. "Not really.''

"Well. At least you're consulting a professional. That would have been my next piece of advice.''

At first, she didn't know what he was talking about, then she realized he thought the psychiatric consultation was regarding Michael's amnesia. "Right,'' she said. "It seemed like the thing to do.''

"Listen. I wasn't going to mention this to you. I mean, nothing came of it, and I didn't want you to worry. But someone was asking questions about your friend at the hospital the other day,'' he said.

Aggie sat bolt upright, every nerve in her body instantly alert. "What? About Michael?''

"That's right. At least we're pretty sure that's who the guy was asking about. The strange thing was, he came straight to the floor, not through Medical Records. He gave the nurses a description and said the patient might be using the name Michael something.''

"Michael *what?*'' She practically screamed it at him. "Do you mean someone came there who knew his last name and you don't remember what it *was?*''

"Hey, don't yell at me. I wasn't even there. The only reason the nurses told me was because one of them remembered he was discharged into your care. And for your information, they didn't tell me the last name, I don't think they knew it. They said 'Michael something.'''

"Okay, okay,'' she muttered. Her mind was racing. "I'll stop by the hospital and find out who the man talked to. So what did they tell him? Who was this person?''

"I'm telling you, I wasn't there.'' David was beginning to sound impatient. "And he didn't leave a card. As for what they told him—nothing, of course. Our policy is very strict. No information is released on any patient without written authorization or a court order. And if it makes you feel any better, I'm not entirely sure this fellow is someone your Michael would want to know. He was referred to Medical Records, but he never showed up there. Sounds kind of sleazy to me. He might be an ambulance chaser, fishing for a client. Or maybe a reporter trying to track down your mystery man. Good column the other day, by the way."

"Thanks," she replied absently. "I guess he could have made up a last name for Michael, just to sound legitimate."

"Probably did."

"But no one told him anything."

"Not a thing."

"Thanks, David. I'll talk to you later."

"Hey, what about dinner?"

"I'll call you," she promised, and hung up the phone.

But first she called Dr. Morrison, and using all of David's influence, got an appointment for Michael ten days hence.

Then she called the third floor of St. Vincent's Hospital and finally tracked down the nurse who had talked to the stranger about Michael. To Aggie's deep disappointment, she remembered nothing about the stranger except that he was blond and very good-looking, had a British accent and that he wore an expensive designer suit and what she described as a "luscious" cologne. No, he hadn't given his name. Nor had he said why he was looking for Michael. As for the last name he had given for Michael, it started with a *K,* she thought, or maybe an *S.* She hadn't really paid attention, she apologized, because she knew she couldn't give out any information. It had been a busy day. She had sent him to Medical Records. Had Aggie tried there?

Aggie did try, just to be on the safe side, but David was right: the stranger had made no attempt to go through legitimate channels. Which meant David was probably right; the man was a sleaze looking for a story or a quick buck and had given up when he couldn't charm his way to the information.

Or he was one of the men who had been chasing Michael.

But even if he was, Aggie assured herself, he had found nothing. He had failed. At any rate, he was long gone by now and they might not ever know who he was or what he had wanted.

It had been a week since the horrifying episode in the middle of the night. Michael had quietly repaired the broken window and, at the same time, installed a new dead bolt—the kind that required a key to be opened from the inside as well as from the outside. The way he handed the key to her without a word broke her heart, and in a stubborn, probably foolish gesture of defiance, she never used the new lock.

Michael went to work every day and stayed late. His skin grew darker and his muscles leaner, and when he came home at night, he could barely stay awake long enough to eat the meal she always had waiting for him. Aggie knew he was trying to work himself into an exhaustion that would prohibit dreams, and perhaps he was succeeding. The past few nights had been quiet.

Still, Aggie had been reluctant to leave the house in case he needed her or, more truthfully, because she was superstitiously afraid that if she was not waiting for him when he came home, he would not come back at all. On Thursdays, however, there was a weekly staff meeting she couldn't get out of. Besides, she had other important business to take care of at the paper.

She had not anticipated how strangely reassuring it would be to step into the real world again. The ordinary hustle and bustle of a big-city newspaper, the interoffice bickering, the smell of stale coffee and newsprint... There was no room for beasts of the night here. No unexplained genetic anomalies, no hallucinatory experiences, no terror of the unknown. Here nothing was real until the city editor declared it to be, and Aggie found it all enormously strengthening.

Still, she was anxious to get home to Michael.

After the meeting, Al draped his arm around her shoulders and walked her back to the City room. "Well, I've got to say, it's working out even better than I hoped. Have you seen the mail you've gotten on last week's column? The reading public is a sap for that kind of sentiment, just like I said they were. Keep it up."

Aggie gave him a dry look. He spoke as though the whole thing had been his idea. "Yes, Chief."

"So what's the word on this fellow, anyway? Any clue as to who he is?"

"Not really."

He nodded approvingly. "Good. I figure we can stretch this out over a month, six weeks, easily. Fantastic. Great for circulation."

Aggie missed a step, staring at him. Could it have been only a few weeks ago that she herself had voiced that sentiment? Could she possibly ever have been that shortsighted?

She said brusquely, "I have to see someone in Research. I'll talk to you later, Al."

She left him more or less gaping at her abrupt departure.

There was no question in her mind about sharing with Al her plan for tracking down Michael's identity; as far as he was concerned—and he had gotten the idea from her—the longer Michael remained a mystery man, the better. She therefore went to one of the best researchers she knew, and was glad that Martha owed her a favor.

"Look, it's not like I'm asking you to get me AP photos of a bull elephant giving birth on Madison Avenue," she cajoled. "It's just one itty-bitty emblem. Put it in the computer, it'll take you half an hour to track down."

Martha wheeled back from her desk, thrust her glasses up into her hair and regarded Aggie dryly. "In your dreams, girlfriend."

The woman stretched to the worktable adjacent to her computer station and picked up a stack of folders eighteen inches thick. "This is just what I have to get out by Sunday. And not a single solitary one of them has anything to do with any obscure runic symbols that you'd have to have a data base the size of East Africa to track down."

Aggie decided not to waste time with the direct approach. She affected a pained sigh. "Well, I can understand being busy. I guess you could say it's a good thing I wasn't too busy to keep the boss off your trail the day your cat had kittens and you had to rush her to the vet for a cesarian, huh?"

Martha scowled. "Hey, I offered you a kitten, didn't I?"

Aggie leaned over the desk again. "Oh, come on, Martha, at least look at what I've got."

"I don't have to. I know what you *haven't* got. And that's a name, a place, a category, a date, and those are the *only* criteria my computer knows how to search by."

"Well, couldn't you do it without the computer this once?"

Martha looked at her as though she had lost her mind.

"Not even for a potential Russian prince?"

"Not even for a *guaranteed* Russian prince."

Once again, Aggie gave an exaggerated sigh. "All right, Martha, thanks, anyway. I'll tell him. But he's going to be awfully disappointed."

She started toward the door.

"Hey, wait a minute."

When she turned back, Martha had wheeled her chair around her desk and was looking very interested. "This is for that guy you've been writing about, right? The Mystery Man."

"Michael," Aggie corrected. She was getting a little annoyed at hearing him referred to by that phrase.

She grinned. "Say, is he as adorable as he sounds?"

"Dark and enchanting," Aggie assured her.

"Boy, would I like a chance to meet someone like that."

"He's taking me to the Francetta Gallery opening tonight. Do this for me and I'll see what I can do to get you an invitation."

Martha made a face. "If I do this for you, I'll be

up all night trying to make up for the time I've lost. Let me see what you've got.''

Aggie hurried over to Martha's desk, removing from her purse the folded paper upon which she had made a drawing of the medallion Michael wore.

"You see?'' she explained. "It's a half-shaded circle, like a shadowed moon. Maybe it's some kind of religious symbol—I don't know, good and evil, the dual nature of man. Maybe it's part of a family crest, an old-world name. Maybe it's a corporate logo.''

"It does look familiar,'' Martha admitted.

"I thought so, too,'' Aggie agreed.

And then Martha shrugged. "On the other hand, it's not exactly one of your more complicated designs. It could mean anything. Or nothing.''

"He wears it on a medallion. There's an inscription on the back,'' Aggie offered helpfully. "'To Michael the First, From All of Us.'''

"Which means it could be just a piece of pretty jewelry.''

"Anything you could find out,'' Aggie said sincerely, "would mean a lot to me.''

Now it was Martha's turn to sigh. "I don't know how I let myself get talked into these things.''

Aggie grinned and hugged her colleague's shoulders. "What's your favorite wine? There will be a bottle of it waiting for you to get home tonight.''

"Get out of here,'' Martha grumbled. "I've got work to do.''

Aggie practically skipped toward the door.

"Dewars!'' Martha called after her.

Aggie turned with her hand on the doorknob. "That's a scotch.''

"You got it, kid.''

Aggie grinned and made a circle with her thumb and forefinger, then left the office.

For the first time in days, she felt hopeful.

In the newsstand in the lobby downstairs, Noel folded the magazine he had been perusing and left the building. He did not need to wait for Aggie to come downstairs. He had not needed to follow her up, and he had no intention of following her home. Everything he needed from her, he had already learned, and he would see her again soon enough.

He had good ears, almost as good as Michael's. They had served him well in eavesdropping on the nurse's conversation after he left the floor at St. Vincent's, which was how he had learned about Aggie McDonald in the first place. It hadn't been hard to track her down, and when he'd called her paper, ostensibly for an appointment, they had told him that she worked at home but could be expected in on Thursdays. From there, it was only a matter of waiting. After all, her picture was featured every week right next to her column in the paper.

He hadn't read her column, although the conversation he had just overheard made him think it might be a good idea for him to do so. There were other things in the conversation he would have to analyze and try to put into context, too. What, for example, was she doing with Michael's medallion? What was *Michael* doing?

Well, no matter. His questions would all be answered tonight at the Francetta Gallery, and as soon as they were, he could be out of this miserable city and on his way home.

He had only a couple of obstacles to overcome. The

first was to keep Gavin out of the way. The second was to get himself invited to the opening. Fortunately, he was not without contacts in the art world, even the art world of Seattle.

Stepping out into the semisunshine of a busy afternoon, Noel shot his cuffs and straightened his tie as he looked around for a cab. Finding none, he decided to walk across the street to the Hyatt for a cup of tea, and from there to make his phone calls. He whistled a little tune under his breath as he started down the street, feeling cheerier than he had in weeks.

CHAPTER TWELVE

The tuxedo, despite the fact that it was rented, felt like a second skin. Michael looked at himself in the mirror and he felt an enormous sense of familiarity, reassurance, as a collage of impressions flashed across his mind. Graceful bare shoulders in a Dior gown, gleaming marble floors, the clink of Steuben crystal, a string quartet playing Vivaldi, the salty taste of caviar on his tongue, the silk of a good wine, well-known faces, famous smiles. He thought, *This is where I belong,* and at almost the same moment, in a flash of confusion, *No, that's where I belong...*

And even though the images that cluttered his mind were uncertain, there was enormous comfort in their presence. No one, he reasoned with a welcome spark of his old dry humor, who tied a bow tie with the ease he demonstrated could possibly have any relationship to the cretinous beast he had imagined himself to be.

Aggie was waiting for him in the living room of her house, and he entered after a soft knock. The sight of her took his breath away.

She was wearing a black chiffon gown with a spray of rhinestones diagonally across the bodice and on the one shoulder strap. The soft material hugged her waist and her hips and dropped into filmy handkerchief pleats below her black-stockinged calves. Her pumps were black satin and she carried a small black evening purse. There were small diamonds in her ears and a glittering necklace around her neck.

He wanted to scoop her up and press her to him, melting into her, drowning in her loveliness. He deliberately did not move.

She looked anxious and unsure until he spoke.

"Aggie," he said softly. "You are the picture of elegance and beauty."

She relaxed, and made a casual gesture toward the jewelry. "It's all fake," she said.

He laughed, and offered his arm. "I wouldn't have known. The sophisticated look suits you."

Aggie placed her hand on his arm and felt a thrill at his nearness, at the feel of his strong arm beneath the fine material. Michael in a tuxedo took her breath away. His skin was a golden contrast against his crisp white shirtfront, his eyes a deep sun-washed blue. He had braided his hair and tucked it into a tight double knot against the back of his collar, and the effect was to give him a courtly, old-world look. He was tall and strong and he made her feel dainty and feminine. He was smooth and urbane and he made her feel glamorous. She was proud to be seen with him, excited to be near him and happy, for the moment, to pretend that nothing disturbing had ever happened between them. He made it easy to pretend.

The opening was well attended, and immediately as they stepped inside the door, Michael was suffused with the scents of chafing dishes, candle wax and intermingled perfumes, a dozen of them, a hundred, all of them heady and familiar and welcoming. His ears easily separated the murmur of several dozen voices into individual conversations, but they did not interest him and he let the sound fade into a pleasant buzz backed by the strains of a Celtic harp situated in the upper gallery. It was the scents that described the night for him, and he took a moment to savor them.

Oil paint and fixative, carpenter's glue, new carpet. Sauvignon blanc, 1991, California vintage. Brie, softening to room temperature. Human sweat, delicate and sweet, good cotton, new satin, dry-cleaning fluid. And something else, something that made the small hairs on the back of his neck prickle, and he couldn't exactly say why. It was a familiar scent, but one he couldn't describe. It was a good scent—and a dangerous one. He knew it, he welcomed it, he knew he should avoid it. What *was* it? He looked around, frowning a little, but saw nothing that might account for the odd sensation of recognition he felt. Perhaps he was mistaken. There were, after all, so many other delightful sensory stimulations competing for his attention.

Aggie paused and lifted her hand to someone in the crowd. Someone else was making her way over to them. He knew their entrance had caused quite a stir, and he knew why. Aggie was stunning.

She grinned up at Michael. "I apologize for showing you off," she said, "but I don't think I've ever had such a good-looking date before."

His hand had been on her back, now it moved up to possessively, affectionately stroke the bare part between her shoulder blades. He smiled as he replied, "I'm sure I never have."

Aggie pressed her head playfully against his shoulder and murmured, "If I were a kitten, I would purr."

That made him laugh and he dropped his hand to her waist. A plump matron in a green dress and emerald ring to match begged to be introduced, and he liked the way Aggie's hand curled around his arm as she introduced him as, "My friend Michael."

The matron eyed him up and down and melted into blushes when he bent over her hand, exclaiming, "My dear, he is adorable! Where in the world did you find him?"

Aggie's eyes danced as she replied, "I picked him up on the street, actually."

Michael knew then that no matter how many hundreds of events like this there had been in a life he no longer remembered, this was the only one that would ever matter. Because this was the only one he had ever attended with Aggie.

They moved from room to room and every few steps someone else would come up to introduce himself or asked to be introduced. Aggie swelled with pride every time she said his name, was bathed in wonder and admiration as she watched the ease with which he interacted with perfect strangers—politicians, social snobs, dilettantes, members of the press— as though he had been born to them, which to anyone with half an eye it was clear that he had. His assessment of the artwork was knowledgeable and astute, and delivered with just enough charm to have Olivetta Francetta, the gallery owner, all but drooling at his feet. Aggie watched him move from person to person, masterpiece to masterpiece, and her heart clenched with tenderness and longing, and she thought, *Oh, Michael, don't you see who you are, what you are? How could you ever have thought you were less? What must have happened to you, to make you doubt your own sanity...to make me doubt it?*

Carl Fromer, the art critic from a rival paper, sidled up next to her. He had a cocktail napkin overflowing with hors d'oeuvres in one hand and a brimming glass of wine in the other; when he gestured, it was with his shoulder. "Quite a catch, McDonald," he said, indicating Michael with a twist of his shoulder. "Who did you say he was?"

Across the room, Michael caught her eye and lifted his glass to her, just slightly. The gesture was as intimate as a kiss.

Aggie sipped from her own glass, watching Michael across its rim. "His name is Michael," she said. "He's new in town."

And watching him, she knew the answer to the question she had been afraid to ask herself these past weeks. Why she had disregarded all common sense and welcomed him into her home. Why she trusted him when all evidence indicated she do exactly the opposite. Why she couldn't be afraid of him, no matter how often she was tempted to. It was really very simple.

"And? That's it? That's all you know about him?" Carl asked.

"Pretty much," she agreed. Except that he was the man she had been waiting for. The only man she had ever known with whom she could honestly try to share her life. The man she wanted to father her children.

Catching Michael's eye again, she smiled, and sipped from her glass.

Aggie's smile was like a magnet, beckoning him. Michael turned to excuse himself from the group with which he had been standing, when something caught his attention.

"Honesty," he murmured.

The woman who had just come to stand next to him looked startled. "Excuse me?"

"Your perfume," he said. "It's Honesty."

It was sweet and certain, strangely disorienting, bringing with it a jumble of confused impressions and almost-memories... *Honesty*. Home.

She laughed. "My dear, you're right! You *are* good! It's a brand-new fragrance, do you love it?" She turned her head as though actually expecting him to sniff behind her ear.

He said, "It's very nice." And though he wanted to stand near, inhaling the perfume and letting its fragrance release the flood of memories he could feel pressing against the gate of his mind, there was something else.

The perfume was cloying, overpowering. Yet just beneath it, almost disguised by it, was another scent. Something alarming, something close. Inside, he felt a building urgency, a need to be away from here. He managed a vague smile around the group. "Excuse me, please."

He had taken two steps, when that scent reached him again and he knew what the perfume had disguised. The danger smell, the good-bad smell, the sense-confusing smell. He edged his way through the crowd, looking for Aggie, and the scent grew stronger. It was behind him.

He turned abruptly and was face-to-face with a tall, blond man with ice green eyes. The man said pleasantly, "Hello, Michael."

Michael's heart began to pound. He knew this man...and he didn't. His scent was suffocating, reminding Michael of a jumble of things and none of them made sense: ice and stone, laughter and good wine, faces at a dinner table, fear in the night, running, blood on the leaves...

Michael forcibly maintained the man's gaze, he made his heartbeat slow. He said, "I'm sorry. Have we been introduced?"

The green eyes narrowed just fractionally, then cleared. He laid his hand on Michael's arm, not a threatening gesture or a controlling one, but not entirely friendly, either. "I see we have some things to talk about," the man said quietly.

Michael pulled his arm away. "I don't know you, sir. And there's nothing I care to discuss with you. Excuse me, please."

He left the other man looking too stunned to respond, and the moment he made his escape, the urgency started filling his throat again, pounding in his chest, breaking out in fine beads of sweat beneath his shirt. He could feel it behind him: danger. He could smell it following him: danger. He pushed through the bodies blocking him and his ears were filled with their nonsensical chatter, the thunder of his own pulse and another pulse behind him, equally fast, equally strong.

He found Aggie, closed his hand around her arm. "We have to leave," he said hoarsely.

She looked startled. "Michael, what's wrong? Are you sick?"

"Hurry!"

She tried to protest but he pulled her away, moving toward the exit, and even then he knew it was too late. Without warning, the man stepped in front of him again. He said, "Michael, I just want to talk. You know, if I found you once, I can do it again, so you may as well talk to me now."

If it hadn't been for Aggie, he could have made his

escape. But Aggie stopped dead still, staring at the stranger. Michael knew he had no choice but to deal with him. Hopefully, he would be able to do so in a civilized manner.

He slid his arm around Aggie's waist, the better to keep her close if they should have to run. He said, quietly and deliberately, "I don't know you. I have nothing to say to you. I'm afraid I must ask that you stop harassing me. You're upsetting the lady."

The other man's eyes flickered briefly to Aggie without interest, then back to Michael. His gaze was probing, only half disbelieving. "You really don't recognize me, do you?" he said.

Aggie burst out, "Do you know him?"

Michael's hand tightened warningly on Aggie's waist. "No," he said coldly. "He doesn't know me."

Amazement crossed the blond man's face. "Genuine amnesia? You really don't remember? How fascinating!"

"I don't want to have a scene here. Leave us alone," Michael warned.

The other man insisted impatiently. "Michael, for God's sake, it's Noel! Your cousin!"

Michael turned Aggie quickly toward the door. "Let's go."

Aggie cried, "Michael!"

The blond man blocked his way once again. Reaching into the collar of his dress shirt, he extracted a gold chain, swinging the pendant it supported before Michael's face. "Look!" he demanded. "You know it's true. I can help you, but you've got to—"

Michael whirled, pulling Aggie with him, and rushed toward the door. He put one startled body after another between them and the stranger, overpowering

Aggie's lagging, protesting steps, until they pushed out into the night.

"Michael, what are you doing?" she cried, twisting away from him. "Didn't you see? He had a medallion just like yours! He knows who you are, Michael!"

"I know." He was breathing hard as he grabbed her hand again, scanning the traffic. "For God's sake, hurry! He's right behind us!"

Some of his urgency must have finally communicated itself to her because when the break came in the traffic, she was ready and they dashed across the street to the garage where they had left her car.

The garage was a self-park facility. It was too late for office workers to be claiming their cars and too early for party and theatergoers to be returning; the garage was deserted. Their footsteps clattered eerily on the empty concrete, their rushing breaths echoed.

"Michael, I don't understand," Aggie gasped. "That man—did you know him? Was he—"

"I think so." He pulled her toward the stairs that led to the second level where her car was parked.

"But he didn't look like—how could he—"

"I don't know, Aggie, I don't know." His voice was tight and desperate. "But he's not far behind us so just hurry, please."

Aggie's head was spinning. None of it made sense. What had started out as the most perfect evening of her life had suddenly, inexplicably turned into a James Bond-type drama. How could she ever have gotten involved in this? What was she doing fleeing blindly through a parking garage in her evening clothes from a man who might be the answer to all her questions— or from a determined killer? She needed to stop and think, she needed to talk to Michael. How could this be happening?

And then she remembered the man who had been asking questions at the hospital. He had been described as blond and good-looking, with a British accent. It couldn't be just a coincidence. It had to be the same man.

She caught Michael's arm for balance as they reached the second level and spun around to face him. "Michael, listen. That man, I think I know—"

It all happened in an instant. She saw something change in Michael's face as he looked over her shoulder, a flash of shock or terror. In the same instant, there was a sound—a growl or a roar that echoed through the empty garage and turned Aggie's blood to ice. Before she could draw a breath or turn her head, Michael grabbed her shoulders and flung her away from him, hard, so hard that her hip bounced off the adjacent wall and she hit the concrete floor with enough force to knock the breath out of her.

It seemed an eternity that she lay there, gasping for air and drawing in nothing, while the horror unfolded before her. A man came from nowhere, lunging at Michael, and it *wasn't* the blond man from the party, it was someone else, and suddenly she knew they had walked—no, run—into a trap. He had scraggly brown hair and a scruffy beard and when he charged at Michael, he made a sound, that roaring sound that was like the loosened hounds of hell.

Michael only had time to throw up his hands to shield his face before the man was upon him, and still Aggie couldn't scream, couldn't breathe. The attacker held something aloft in his hand, and it wasn't until a sharp red line appeared on the white cuff of Michael's shirt that Aggie realized the object was a knife.

Then her breath came back in a rush and she tried to scream but all that came out was a muffled, choked cry. The man brought the knife down again and Michael was on his knees; she couldn't see him. She tried to scramble to him on her hands and knees, and then she heard something else. Through the sound of her own ragged sobs, through the roar of terror in her ears, through the savage animal-sounds the attacker was making, she heard a low and vicious, hackle-raising growl, the scuttle of claws on concrete. She shrank back in terror as the biggest dog she had ever seen flashed across her range of vision and launched itself at the attacker.

Less than thirty seconds had passed since Michael had first seen his assailant. He had no time to think, no time to wonder, no time to analyze. Pain stung his hands and arms from the blade of the knife, sharpening his instincts and quickening his reactions. He had one hand around the throat of the attacker and the other on the wrist that held the knife. He could feel his body begin to change, and then the wolf was upon them.

The attacker was pulled backward, off of Michael, torn from his grip. It was quick, too quick, strong and sure. A growl of protest rumbled in his throat, low and primitive and completely uncontrollable.

He saw his assailant was no longer a man but a half-changed man—bones shifting and tissue transforming as it struggled to take on its natural shape as the wolf attacked him. But it was too late. The wolf's teeth were sharp and sure. Michael felt the pull of violence in his belly, the need to fight, the need to *change*...

It was a familiar sensation now, the prickling of his

skin, the aching of his joints, the stretching of his bones and the fire burning in his brain. It was out of control, consuming him, the smell of fear, the taste of death, the need for defense, and suddenly, unexpectedly, a rush of understanding, of *clarity,* the memory of horror.

It all took place in seconds. The attack, the killing, the need…and the scream.

Aggie's cry, calling to him; Aggie's fear, reaching him; Aggie's need, pulling him back.

He spun around and saw the wolf straddling the lifeless body of the attacker, its eyes glinting a challenge, its teeth bared and ready. There was an instant in which he wavered, in which he stared into the eyes of the wolf and reality blurred before him, the consciousness he knew as a man started to slip away, and then he heard Aggie's sob again. He turned to her.

She was on the floor, her back against the wall and her knees drawn up to her chest. Both hands were across her mouth, smothering the cries of terror that were her every breath. Not for all his life could Michael have left her like that. He was with her in an instant, scooping her against him, shielding her with his strength. All the while his eyes defied the wolf.

Aggie threw her arms around Michael's neck, clinging to him, but she didn't take her eyes off the wolf. She knew it was a wolf now and not a giant police dog come to their rescue. Its fur was blond and its eyes were green, and around its neck was a gold chain from which was suspended a hexagonal medallion. The shadowed moon.

The wolf just stood there, its paws astride the lifeless man, its sides heaving, its clever eyes watching. Aggie saw all this but she processed none of it, just as she had seen the changes that had begun to overtake the knife-wielding maniac when the wolf first attacked him. The horribly elongated jaw, the shrinking eyes, the fur-covered hands…she had seen it, but she hadn't believed it.

Then she realized something else. The dead man wore a medallion around his neck, too, just like Michael's.

The wolf took a step toward them and stopped abruptly at a sound from Michael. It was a strange sound, deep in his throat, like a rumble or a growl, so soft that Aggie felt the vibration rather than heard it. But the wolf heard the warning and accepted it for what it was. He backed up, very carefully, on all four paws.

The wolf shook himself then, blond fur shimmering and fluffing in the wind created by his own action. It was a simple thing at first, like a dog shedding water, but then it became faster and more deliberate. Not if she lived a hundred years would Aggie be able to adequately describe what happened next.

Fur rippled and smoothed into flesh, flesh stretched and molded itself into another form; the face shortened and rounded, paws elongated and became fingers and toes. It was an oddly beautiful, intensely compelling thing to watch, not at all the grotesque and painful transformation so often depicted in horror movies. It was an unfolding, a becoming, a wholly natural melting away of one form for the other. Perhaps that was why it did not terrify Aggie. She was shocked, her body went on automatic while her mind struggled to process this incredible thing she had just seen, but she was not afraid.

Fear, no doubt, would come later.

The wolf-creature arched its beautiful back, flexed its arms and legs and shook out its blond mane of hair. Splendidly naked, perfectly formed, it rose to his full human height.

It was the blond man from the party.

His body was sleek with sweat and he was breathing hard, as though he had just run a great distance. But the look in his eye was amused as he glanced at Aggie, the tone of his voice unerringly polite and touched with dryness. ''Madam,'' he said, gesturing to his attire, or lack thereof, ''I apologize.''

His gaze shifted to Michael. ''May I dress?''

Michael said nothing. Aggie felt her frail grip on sanity slipping into an almost hysterical sense of disassociation. She was trembling violently and she couldn't stop, but she was fascinated. She wouldn't have missed this for the world.

The man kept his eyes warily on Michael as he moved away, and when he was out of sight behind the angle of the wall, Michael's grip tightened on Aggie's shoulders and he pulled her to her feet. She was like a rag doll in his arms, her legs sagging and her feet stumbling. Her hands were twisted in his shirtfront and she couldn't let go; when he urged her to walk, she couldn't do that, either. She just clung to Michael and stared at the place where the stranger had disappeared.

He was quick, and before Michael could drag her more than a few steps toward the car, the blond man returned, fastening the button of his black dress pants. He wore no shoes and he murmured as he approached. ''I must have left my shirt and jacket on the ground floor. I'll have to go back.''

He looked at Michael, though he stopped well away from them. ''We don't have long,'' he said. His breathing was still somewhat labored from exertion, though he controlled it well. "We have to get this mess cleaned up before someone comes along."

The bizarre glint of humor in his eyes was gone now; his expression was deadly serious. "I had to do it, you know. He broke the law. He attacked in human form and you know he would have killed you if he could have."

As he spoke, he gestured toward the body and Aggie's eyes were irresistibly drawn there. A cry caught in the back of her throat. The man who had lain there only moments ago was gone. In his place was the lifeless body of a rangy brown wolf. The gold medallion was still around its neck.

The blond man went on, watching Michael carefully, "I can't fight again tonight, you know that. If you try to leave, I can't stop you. But it won't be over."

A fine note of desperate determination came into his voice and he took a small step forward. "There'll be others, and God knows where it will lead. You'll be on the run for the rest of your life, Michael. The family will be torn apart, our entire heritage in jeopardy. Don't do this to us, to yourself. Come home with me now."

Michael said nothing. He moved against Aggie, urging her to walk, and her legs collapsed. In a single fluid motion and without taking his eyes off the other man, Michael swept her into his arms, close against his chest, and carried her to the car. The blond man made no move toward them, but simply stood there, looking speculative and alert.

Michael snatched the keys from her evening bag and put her in the car, pushing her across to the passenger seat. In only seconds, he was inside, the doors were locked and the engine was roaring.

The car screeched out of the garage, and when Aggie looked back, both the blond man and the body of the wolf were gone. Only a stain of blood remained on the concrete to testify that any of it had ever happened.

CHAPTER THIRTEEN

Michael locked the doors and closed the draperies while Aggie sat on the sofa, shivering. She wasn't aware that she was shivering. She wasn't aware of much of anything until Michael knelt beside her and pushed a brandy snifter into her hand. It was then that she noticed his torn clothes, his bloodstained shirt.

"Michael, you're hurt!" Incipient shock vanished in a rush of concern for him. She struggled to get to her feet. "Let me—"

Gently he pushed her down again. "In every crisis since I've known you, you've taken care of me. Let me take care of you now. The cuts are shallow. I'm not hurt."

She shuddered violently then, remembering, and he lifted the glass to her lips.

"Drink," he commanded.

"What is it?"

"Amaretto. I couldn't find any brandy."

She murmured, "I used it to make a cake once."

"Drink this. Drink it all."

She took a healthy swallow and her eyes burned. It tasted like brandied cherries. Michael pressed the glass to her lips again, and she took another swallow. Her ears buzzed.

She pushed the glass away and Michael set it on the table beside her. He took one of her hands in his, chafing it briefly. His eyes were hollow-rimmed, his face tormented. Wearily, he bowed his head over her hand. "Oh, Aggie," he said raggedly. "What have I done? What kind of madness have I brought into your life?"

She lifted a hand to stroke his hair but he got to his feet abruptly, walking away from her toward the window. "He'll come here, you know," he said. His voice was flat. He lifted the curtain a fraction and peered out, then let it drop again. "The water won't protect me anymore. He used his logic, not his senses, to find me. Grand-père always said our ability to think was the one weapon no one could ever take away from us."

Aggie's heart was beating hard, even through the anesthesia of alcohol. So much, there was so much… "Who is Grand-père?" she asked.

He turned and looked at her for a moment as though the words she spoke were in a foreign language. Then he shook his head, pressing his fingers to his forehead briefly. "It's still foggy. I'm not sure."

In a rapid-fire freeze-frame, Aggie saw the events of the past two hours. Man and wolf, wolf and man, knives and medallions, blood and thunder. A killing…

"Police," she said dully. As though she were moving underwater, she turned and fumbled for the telephone she thought was on the end table beside her. It wasn't. She tried not to panic. "We have to call the police."

"And tell them what?" The incredulity in Michael's voice was like a bark. "Can you honestly picture yourself telling the police what you just saw?"

"What *did* I see?" Aggie cried. Hysteria was swirling around her like ashes in the wind, thickening the air, obscuring her vision. "For God's sake, Michael, what is *happening?*"

Michael spun suddenly and began to pace. "I've got to get out of here," he said tightly, almost to himself. "But what if he comes for you? How do I know he won't? I don't know these people, I don't know what they're capable of. Why can't I *remember?*" Again he pressed his hands to his head angrily, desperately.

But Aggie heard only one thing, and it was enough to propel her off the sofa, to send her stumbling toward Michael. "You're not leaving me!" she cried. She grabbed his arms. "You're not leaving, do you hear?"

He caught her hands and pulled himself from her grip, his face anguished. "Aggie, don't you know what I am? Didn't you see? For the love of God, don't you understand yet?"

"No! I didn't see anything! That wasn't you, you're not like that, it doesn't have anything to do with you! Michael, don't look at me like that! Listen to me!"

But he walked away from her, and when she tried to follow, he flung out an arm to stop her. The last thing she saw in his eyes was pity, and sorrow.

He paced the length of the small room, swung around, and measured its width. From the opposite window, he turned and faced her. His breathing was quick, his expression tight. He forcefully unclenched his fists at his sides. The way he opened his palms looked like a gesture of entreaty, but he could have been merely flexing his hands. Bloodstained cuffs. Torn jacket. Haunted eyes.

He said, "I remember some of it. What we are. What I ran from. The change."

He drew a deep, ragged breath, turning his gaze slightly upward, just avoiding her eyes. "I wanted to live like a human, and they wouldn't let me. I wanted to *be* human...but I'm not."

She whispered, "Michael." Gripping the back of a chair that separated them, she took a step toward him.

He held up a hand to stay her. His eyes grew unfocused and his gaze seemed to turn inward as the words came tumbling out, uncensored memories one after another. "Not human at all," he said. "Half human, half wolf, looking like both at times but not like either one, not really. Better. Stronger, smarter, faster, bred to survive…oh, we're a very old species. Once we lived openly among you. Centuries ago, we were hunted, persecuted, driven underground, but we survived. Not only survived but prospered. Now we live with you, have commerce with you, pass for you most of the time. But we can't deny our nature, and to stay in human form too long is…" Now he hesitated, seeming unsure of the word. "Taboo. Unhealthy. To grow too attached to the human world is considered a sign of weakness, especially if you're…" He caught his breath, remembering. "If you're next in line to…to rule."

He looked at her slowly, uncertainty mixed with wonder in his eyes. "That was me. I had the keys to the kingdom in my hand…and I didn't want them. I wasn't interested in the old ways, I didn't want the power. I wanted to live a human life." And he dropped his eyes. "But I couldn't. Because I'm not human."

Suddenly, he turned back to the window, agitated again. "He was right. They'll never let me go. They can't. They will be chasing me for the rest of my life. Because I have to die or be defeated in battle before another heir can be named. They'll come for me, and if they find me here, I don't know that I can protect you—"

"Michael, stop it." She gripped the back of the chair, fingernails digging in, trying to control her quick, staccato breathing and the panic that choked in her chest. "Just stop it, stop the crazy talk, stop looking at me like that."

Fiercely, she pushed her hands through her hair, grasping for logic, desperately searching for the last few threads of her rapidly unraveling world. "Look, what happened with those others, it was bizarre, it was incredible, but it wasn't *you*. It had nothing to do with you."

Swiftly he was beside her, the medallion clenched in his fist. "Don't you see? Half dark, half light. Half wolf, half man, never to forget we have to respond to the ancient call of the moon—"

"It means nothing. It's a trick, just—"

"That night," he said quietly as his eyes searched her face with burning intensity, probing certainty, "I wanted to make love to you, and I started to change... because *we can't make love in human form*. We weren't meant to mate with humans, we can't—"

"Stop it!" She covered her ears with her hands. "Stop it. This is insane. Why are you doing this?"

He took her wrists and pulled her hands from her ears. Never had she seen such sorrow in a man's face, such anguish in his eyes. "Because," he answered simply, "I promised to tell you the truth."

She turned her hands to his, holding his arms, holding his gaze desperately, searchingly. "You're not one of them," she whispered. "You're not."

He tried to pull away, but her grip intensified, her voice strengthened. "Michael, listen to me, we can get help for you, this doesn't have to be—"

"Aggie, please..."

"Don't do this to me, Michael." Until that moment, she had been unaware that her face was wet with tears. She held on to his arms fiercely. "I've waited too long for you, I'm not going to lose you! I love you, Michael, don't you know that? I love you, and I'm not going to lose you!"

She saw the shock in his eyes, but not before she saw the leap of welcome; she saw the tightening of his lips, but not before she saw the longing. He gripped her shoulders. Hard. He said with low, intense ferocity, "You can't love me. I can't love you. I can never be your lover. I can't be part of your world. I can't love you, Aggie. Damn it, I can't!"

But then his mouth was on hers, and her heart, her spirit, her entire being leaped to meet him. The kiss they shared was fierce and intense, fingers gripping and bruising, mouths opening and pressing as though seeking to drink in the very life's fluid of the other. Aggie tasted his longing and was filled with desperation and she knew, even as some small part of her, hidden far back in the secret recesses of her mind, must have known all along. She inhaled the rich feral scent of him, twisted her hands in the heavy lengths of his hair, arched her neck to the press of his teeth and she knew; she knew and she gloried in it.

Michael understood what it was like to be torn in two. Surrender warred with need; he knew what he risked, but it was worth it, worth anything for one more taste of her, one more moment to hold her in his arms and pretend, with all the blind desperation of any lover who had ever lived, that she could be his. She was the flame and he was the fire; they flowed into each other and became an inferno consuming everything in their path: air, matter, reason, control...

He knew he tempted fate and perhaps he did it deliberately. Perhaps some dark and secret part of him needed to prove to her and to himself what he knew the truth to be. The only thing he knew for certain with the last reasoning part of his mind was that he could not live without her, that without her there was no life, that with his very last breath he wanted her. And by the time the savagery started to rise, the change had him in its grip and it was too late.

Michael pushed her away from him with a cry that sounded like a roar to his ears. He stumbled backward, covering his face with his hands and he knew from the horror he saw in hers that already he had begun to change. The tingling, burning in his skin, the aching in his joints, the clawing, raging animal inside bursting to get out... He tried, but he couldn't control it, didn't *want* to control it; it was too late. Too late, and all he could do was surrender.

Aggie stumbled back, her hand pressed to her mouth to suppress screams as she watched the impossible unfold before her. His face...his face was changing, drenched with sweat, wrenched in agony as it became longer, darker, smoother, but his eyes remained the same and she had never seen such pain, such anger and pleading and helplessness. She wanted to run to him and even took a step toward him, but he flung out an arm to stop her, and a lamp exploded on the floor.

She shrank back as he cried out suddenly—not a cry, but a roar, a reverberating sound of savagery and triumph—and he turned his head to the ceiling, sinking to his knees. He tore at his clothing and it came apart in shreds. He left red claw marks on his perspiration-slick skin, but they quickly faded beneath the thickening of hair, the toughening of flesh. Shirt, jacket, trousers, shoes were flayed into ribbons and cast aside like bothersome bits of tissue.

Aggie stepped backward until she was against the wall, and then she gripped the unyielding plaster as though mere force of will could make it dissolve and allow her egress. She did not realize that the high rhythmic sound in her ears was the sound of her own tiny gasping sobs, for these reactions were only physical, unpreventable, having little, if anything, to do with her. Her mind, her *soul* was mesmerized by what she saw unfolding before her, by the hot electric smell of magic that permeated the small room, by the power of miraculous transmutation that was taking place before her.

Energy seemed to swirl around him in sparks and waves as the magnificent creature that was Michael stretched himself to his full height, arms uplifted, head thrown back. Hands into paws, arms into forelegs, hair into shimmering, silky fur. Chest, haunches, tail, spinning flesh into flesh, muscle into muscle, life into life. The wolf, perfect and fully formed, dropped to all fours and turned to face her.

Michael's eyes, filled with anguish, Michael's voice, roaring with pain. And suddenly, it was not Michael, but a wild animal trapped in a small space, crazed and terrified. It spun around and, with a roar, raced toward the French door.

Aggie screamed, "Michael!"

But it was too late. He threw himself against the closed door and glass exploded outward. The wolf struck the stone patio and lay there, lifeless, in a pool of broken glass.

Cotton sheets against his skin. The sting of abrasions on his hands and feet. Something warm against his shoulder. The smell of Aggie. He lay in that gentle limbo for a timeless eternity, feeling nothing, knowing nothing except the nearness of her. And then the memories came and he couldn't stop them. He groaned softly and opened his eyes.

Her head lay against his shoulder, as though she had fallen asleep while keeping watch over him. She had changed from her black evening dress into a faded pink, often-washed nightshirt; her hair gleamed like a new penny against the pillow, her lashes formed crescent shadows on her ivory skin. He could see, where the long shirt rode up, the edge of her panties, the curve of a slender thigh. She was everything good and innocent, perfect and unflawed in all the world. He wanted to keep her there forever, just as she was, and look at her.

But his movement had disturbed her. She opened her eyes and was instantly aware. "Oh, Michael, thank God." She sat up, brushing a cool hand across his forehead. "I was so worried."

He was naked beneath the sheets, he could smell the iodine she had used on his cuts. He tried to piece together a picture of what had happened after the change, but it was not something he really wanted to know.

His voice was husky, and the first few words were slurred. "How did you..." He cleared his throat and tried again. "How did you get me here?"

She took a glass of water from the bedside table and offered it to him. He eased himself to a sitting position and drank, thirsty.

"You were conscious before, don't you remember?" she said. "After—after you went through the door, you changed back, involuntarily, I think. I was so scared. I thought you were dead. But I felt a pulse and—and you finally came around but your eyes were—oh, God, Michael, you didn't recognize me! I got you back inside and cleaned your wounds, but you kept drifting in and out of consciousness. I was afraid to call David, but I didn't know what to do for you. And then finally, you seemed to be sleeping normally and I thought you might be all right... You are, aren't you? Michael, please tell me you're all right!''

He set the empty glass on the table and briefly covered her hand with his. ''I'm sorry, Aggie,'' he said without looking at her. ''For all I've put you through.''

But when she tried to enclose his hand in hers, he pulled away and, pretending to examine the cuts and scratches on his arms, tried to smile. ''One thing is certain, isn't it? I can't be trusted around glass doors.''

''Michael.''

The syllables were heavy with tenderness and concern and they broke his heart. But when she lifted a hand to stroke his hair, he pulled away.

The hurt and confusion in her eyes stabbed at him.

''Michael, what's wrong? What have I done?''

He couldn't stand the pain in her face. He couldn't stand the shame of knowing he had caused it. ''For God's sake, Aggie, you saw what happened! You know what I am! How can you look at me? How can—'' His voice choked, and he had to turn away. ''How can you stand to touch me?''

''Oh, Michael.'' Her breath was like a whisper across his shoulder. Lightly, as though afraid of rejection again, her fingers drifted over the shape of his skull in a butterfly caress. And then, gently, she closed her hand upon his upper arm. "Look at me. Please don't turn away."

He made himself return his gaze to her. He could not believe what he saw in her eyes. No revulsion, no fear. Just anxiety, concern for him.

"I know that what you are and what you can do is beyond anything I know. I'm still not sure I believe it, I don't know that I can ever understand it. I said I couldn't be shocked, but I was. Of course I was. But then…" And she dropped her eyes, struggling to explain. "It's *you*, Michael. It's still you. Even in the other form, I could see your eyes…and it was you."

His own horror and shame over what he remembered began to evaporate beneath the wonder of what she was saying. He probed her eyes, searched her face, and though he found no sign of duplicity, he still could not quite believe it.

"You *saw* it," he insisted hoarsely. "How can you not be afraid?"

Her eyes widened slightly, as though in surprise. "I don't know. I was afraid, of course, because it was strange and new and *impossible* and that was terrifying…and thrilling. But, Michael, I don't think you understand what it's like for a human to see you change." Excitement quickened her voice and glowed in her eyes, and her fingers tightened on his wrist. "It's indescribable, it's beautiful, it's—it's almost like *I* was being transported, too, beyond myself. There's nothing scary about it at all. It's magical."

He simply stared at her. "I never knew that. We don't—I've never changed before a human before. I don't think any of us have. Except Noel." He dropped his eyes, remembering that.

But Aggie was oblivious, her voice rich with wonder. "Didn't you notice, when you were watching him change? How did it make you feel?"

"It made me want to change, too," he admitted. "I had to fight to stay in control. It was hypnotic, like a melody that makes you want to dance."

She laughed. "That's right, I can see that. In a way, it was like that for me, too, just watching."

And she sobered. "But you frightened me at first. You were in so much pain, it was awful to watch. And when it was over..."

"It hurts when you try to stop it," he said. "And afterward...I didn't want you to see me like that. I was so ashamed."

Aggie tried to assure him. "A very wise man once told me that the important thing is that we learn to accept all the people we are inside, and be true to them. Maybe that's why you lost your memory, Michael. You couldn't do that."

He looked at her soberly for a long time. "I never wanted this to happen." He sank back against the headboard, pushing his hand through his hair. "All I wanted was a sane and normal life. I never wanted to drag you into this."

"You didn't drag me into it," Aggie said softly. "I came willingly."

The sheet slipped from his waist as he twisted around to face her fully, baring a portion of his hip. He hesitated a moment, half afraid to touch her, and then he took her shoulders in his hands and said, "I told you once that coming here, finding you, was like something I'd dreamed about in another life. And that's what it was. That's *all* it was, all it can ever be. Knowing you...loving you..." The words were hard to say, but once spoken, seemed the most natural thing in the world. "Was the only good thing I've ever known, and more than I deserve. But it was also my punishment, for trying to escape my nature. Because now I have to give you up."

She was already shaking her head, firmly and calmly. She said simply, "That's not going to happen, Michael."

"Please, Aggie, don't make it harder."

Aggie's gaze was steady and clear, unmarred by so much as a flicker of doubt. "I saw someone die tonight," she said. "I saw the man I love attacked by a madman with a knife and twice I saw a miracle. I saw you lying on the patio tonight and I thought I had lost you forever. I never want to feel like that again, not ever."

Her voice had grown high and tight and she drew a quick sharp breath. "I don't know what's in store for us, I don't know what the future holds. I only know that whatever it is, for me, you'll be part of it. I can't let you out of my life, Michael. Please don't push me out of yours."

"Aggie, this is killing me." The words came in a rush of breath, an agony that closed his eyes and tightened his fingers on her shoulders. Without thinking, he gathered her close, holding her against his chest, burying his face in her hair. "How can I let you go? How can I let you stay?"

Her arms wrapped around him in a fierce embrace, her breathing was damp and uneven against his neck. "You don't have a choice." Her voice was thick and muffled. He could feel her tears. "Not tonight."

"Aggie, don't." He wanted to push her away but he couldn't. His hand molded her scalp, he breathed in the scent of her, fingers thrusting into her hair, drowning in it, storing up sunshine for the long bleak winter ahead. The winter that would last the rest of his life.

She lifted her face to him, eyes glistening, cheeks flushed and wet. She said, "I'm not a fool, Michael. I know what we have to face tomorrow. I don't know what choices we have, what decision we'll make, but tonight, I'm scared and I'm cold and I can't be alone. I don't have to make love with you. I just want to be with you. I just want to be held by you."

He was as helpless as he had ever been with her. He closed his eyes and drew her back into his embrace and descended into the loveliness of her. Aggie. Just to hold her, just to have her near. It was enough.

They sank to the pillow together, wrapped around each other, imbued with the warmth and scent of each other, taking comfort together, growing strong together. He kissed away her tears. She stroked his forehead with a trembling hand. He covered her legs with one of his, drawing her deep into the circle of his body. The sheet slipped away. She caressed the length of his spine. And they held each other, filling themselves with the simple nearness of each other, for a long, long time.

Her breathing grew soft and even; it matched the rhythm of his own. He could feel her heartbeat, and it was inside his chest. He heard the rush of blood through her veins, and it was his own. He did not question the movements of his hands as they moved over her body, caressing her thighs and her satin-clad hips, moving beneath the soft cotton shirt to the bare skin beneath. Her heartbeat quickened. So did his.

She lifted her face to look at him. Her eyes were wide and unafraid. He kissed the corner of her mouth,

gently. Their heartbeats grew quicker, heavier. He
tasted the satiny flesh of her inner lip with his tongue.
He felt her nipples grow hard against his chest.

Her hand moved down, tracing the shape of his back
and his buttocks. He kissed her open mouth, licking
her tongue and her face, tasting her neck. Her heat
rose, penetrating him. Her hand slipped between his
legs, stroking the inside of his thigh. His loins filled
with heat, grew stiff and heavy in the way of human
males, and that was then all he was and all he ever
wanted to be: a human man loving a woman.

It was silent, tender, dreamlike. Later, Aggie would
wonder how it could be, why this time should be so
different from the others, and there would be many
answers, many speculations. For now, all she knew
was the need, basic, primal, unquestioned. It was good,
it was right, it was *necessary* that they become one.
Tonight was all they were promised; tonight might be
forever. And tonight anything was possible.

He caught the edge of her panties and pulled them
down over her knees; she kicked them off the rest of
the way. She moaned out loud as he pushed his hand
between her legs, caressing her. She wrapped her arms
around his neck, sank her teeth into his shoulder. He
pushed her nightshirt up and over her head, pressing
her breasts with his hands, drawing the nipples into
his mouth.

His breath was quick and hot, his heartbeat thunderous. Their perspiration mingled, slickening their
bodies. She wrapped her arms and legs around him,
writhing with need, arching her hips. He took her head
between his hands, his hands wound tightly in her hair
and she saw the savagery of hunger in his eyes, the

intensity of need, and she was afraid—not of him, but of herself and the desperate depths of her own desire.

She felt the stabbing thrust of his penetration and she cried out, arching against him as he filled her. She was dizzy with the force of the sensation, light-headed, weightless, aware of nothing except Michael and the intense, mind-numbing pleasure he created inside her body, the incredible thing that was happening inside her soul. She felt him, not just in the place where their two bodies joined but inside every pore and cell, inside her *mind*. She knew the magic.

She knew what it was to be him, to see with his eyes, to taste with his tongue, to run with his legs. She saw the crystal-blue glacier lake, the jumping stone where he had played as a child. She tasted the crisp clean air with an acuity she had never known in her own body, felt the springiness of grass beneath her feet, the cool splash of water, the sun on her hair. The freedom, the glorious, intoxicating freedom of running, exulting in her own power, glorying in her body, letting the smells of the earth and the air and the wind fill her soul.

She opened her eyes, gasping in wonder, and she saw in Michael's eyes the same kind of joy that she knew and she understood that somehow she was giving back as he gave to her. He had taken her inside himself just as she had taken him, he knew her secrets and her pleasures and he delighted in them, was entranced by them, just as she was by him. This was sharing beyond the human realm. This was love beyond the earthly plane.

They moved together in rhythms that were desperately hypnotic, irresistible and instinctive, and as pleasure spiraled, so did the flow of consciousness between them, memories unwinding like silken threads, sensations shared and amplified for the sharing. She was him. He was her. The beauty of it made her weep.

And she knew the change. In her mind, in Michael's mind, she felt the wonder, the rapture of becoming, of transforming beyond herself, beyond himself. She knew the power and the loss of power, the helplessness, the triumph, the surge of magnificence that allowed her, and him for an instant to touch the face of eternity. The orgasm that gripped her was at first only a reflection of the rapture that had seized her mind and then the two blended, body and soul, an explosion of wonder and breathless, bursting pleasure. She cried out as Michael thrust deep inside her, spilling himself inside her; she held tightly and she wouldn't let him go.

She whispered, ''Michael, Michael...'' as he collapsed atop her, but it was more than a whisper, more than a plea. *Don't let it end, don't leave me, how can I live apart from you?*

And he heard her. He lifted himself, his damp hair streaming over her shoulders, his uneven breath matching the pace of hers. He held her face in his hands and with his eyes he adored her, he promised her, he incited the flame again.

His hands moved beneath her back and they turned in bed until she was astride him. She tasted the salt of his neck, buried her face in his chest, raked her nails along his thighs. She felt him grow strong and hard inside her. He closed his hand on the back of her neck, drawing her down to him. He took the lobe of her ear between his teeth. They thrust together, savagely, fiercely, turning again and again, discovering and rediscovering the ecstasy.

When at last they collapsed, tangled together in exhaustion, they lay for a long time bathed in the glow of the miracle they had created together. There were marks on Aggie's shoulder and neck and breasts from his mouth. His back bore the red lines of her nails. She ached all over. Her hair was soaked and so was his. She could still feel the electric residue of him on her skin, inside her. If her life ended tonight, it would be enough. For this moment, it would be enough.

She threaded her fingers through his wet hair, untangling it. His hand caressed her hip. And at last she had to speak. "Michael," she whispered. "What just happened between us? I mean, *how* did it happen?"

"I don't know." His eyes were beautiful in the lamplight, the color of a glacier lake at sunset. He lifted his hand to stroke her face. "Noel said he couldn't fight again tonight, remember? I think there's a limit to how often we can change within a given time limit. That may be part of it. But the other part is...I wanted it so much. I needed you so much. And..." This seemed difficult for him to articulate; his hand paused in its caress. "I think I never really understood how much choice I really had before."

She looked at him, loving him, aching for him. She didn't know whether or not they would ever be able to recreate what they had just shared, and neither did he. But after this, how could she ever be the same? How could she pretend he had never come into her life?

"Oh, Michael," she whispered breathlessly. She pressed her face into his chest, hugging him tightly. "I can't bear to lose you. Please don't leave me, I don't think I could live without you now..."

He kissed her hair; gently, he lifted her chin so that

she looked at him again. ''I don't think you have a choice,'' he said. ''You see...'' And he dropped a kiss, sweet and tender, on her forehead. ''We mate for life.''

CHAPTER FOURTEEN

It was late morning when Aggie awoke, and a gray drizzle pressed against the windowpane. Michael's face was on the pillow next to hers, his hair tangled over his shoulders, breathing deeply. His arm was heavy across her stomach, but she didn't want to move. She felt warm and pleasantly achy and well loved. The sights and smells of their passion surrounded her like an embrace, the memory had fixed itself into every cell of her being. *Magic,* she thought. *Don't let it end...*

She didn't want to leave him, not even for a moment. She didn't want to get up to face this drab wet day and whatever it might hold. But the call of nature was persistent, and Aggie carefully disentangled herself from Michael's embrace. He barely stirred. He was exhausted. She stood beside the bed for a moment, loving him, aching for him, watching him sleep. Then she turned and padded quietly to the bathroom.

Once up, she was fully awake, and there was no more pretending that she could avoid the morning that had come too quickly. She showered and slipped into jeans and a T-shirt. When she returned to the bedroom, Michael was still sleeping. She decided to let him rest. She smoothed back his hair and kissed him, very lightly, on the forehead. He stirred and reached for her hand. She pressed his fingers gently. "Sleep," she whispered.

She slipped on her sneakers and went into the living

room, closing the bedroom door quietly behind her. She carefully avoided the broken lamp, but there was no ignoring the gaping hole in the glass door. Rain pattered loudly on the patio outside, and she shuddered. More than rain could have come in through that door last night. They had been very, very careless. Michael was right. They had to get out of here. Today.

Suddenly uneasy, she moved to draw the draperies over the French door—a futile gesture, she knew— and then her eye was caught by the blinking light of the answering machine. Someone must have called while they were at the gallery opening...a lifetime ago.

She pressed the button and the message played. "Hey, girlfriend, if all your favors are this easy, I'm going to have to start feeling guilty about that scotch. That logo you gave me belongs to the St. Clare Corporation. Haywood over in Business recognized it right away. According to him, it's some kind of big-deal international company, owns a couple of banks, some audio-design firms, major interests in the giant software companies, stuff like that. But the thing *we* know them for is Clare de Lune Cosmetics—you know, they make that perfume Honesty? Those great magazine ads with guys in the half-unzipped jeans? How about that? Say, do you suppose your fellow could get me some free samples? Of the models, not the perfume. Anyway, Haywood had a prospectus on them, so I faxed you the good parts. Board of directors, major shareholders, that kind of thing. Whatever else you need, you can get from Haywood on Monday. Hope this does it for you."

"God bless you, Martha," Aggie said fervently.

Without even pausing for her umbrella, she dashed

out the kitchen door and across the lawn to the office, flinging open the door, which Michael never remembered to lock. She snatched up the papers from the fax machine and scanned them in the grayish light from the window. Earnings, holdings, offices, *there.* Chairman of the board, Sebastian St. Clare, a broadshouldered, hawk-nosed, foreboding-looking man with a thick mane of snow-white hair and piercing blue eyes. Directors. Division heads. Good God, *Noel Duprey,* vice president in charge of research and development, New Products Division. And there. CEO, Michael St. Clare. Michael of the aristocratic features and quick, sharp eyes, Michael with his thick hair, distinctively streaked with white, tied back at the nape. Dark suit. Harvard tie. *Michael.*

Her knees felt weak. After all this, it was so simple. And after all they had been through, all the shocking, impossible truths they had learned, this was the most stunning. Michael…Clare de Lune…the St. Clare Corporation…*banks,* for God's sake. Her head spun.

She had to tell Michael. She whirled toward the door, papers in hand, and it was over in an instant. A hard arm clamped around her waist. She drew in a breath to scream and tasted cotton and chemicals, and a black cloud came down and swallowed her whole.

Noise. What was that noise? A thrumming, drumming, groaning sound, throbbing in time to the pain in her head. Aggie groaned and opened her eyes fuzzily.

She was in a small room decorated in wine red. The color hurt her eyes. She lay on a narrow sofa with a plush cushion under her head and a silky wool throw covering her legs. There were curtains at one end of the room and curtains over the windows—wine red. There was an oval door with a lever-type handle on the opposite wall.

An attractive blond-framed face came into her field of vision, concerned green eyes looked down at her. "How are you?" he inquired in that smooth Oxford accent. "Do you feel all right?"

The sudden leap of alarm stabbed pain into her head and she groaned again, struggling to sit up. It was him. The man from the garage. Noel.

He took her arm and assisted her to sit. She tried to pull away but was too weak and disoriented.

"Bloody stuff, chloroform," he said. His expression was still concerned. "Damned unpredictable, not that I've had much opportunity for comparison shopping. You aren't going to be sick, are you? These carpets are the very devil to clean."

She pressed her fingers to her forehead and muttered thickly, "My head."

"Shall I fetch you some aspirin?"

She nodded and he patted her knee, getting to his feet.

The moment he was out of sight, she gathered all her strength and bolted toward the door. Her head screamed. She almost had her hand on the handle, when he stepped in front of her, firmly placing his hands on her shoulders, and moved her aside.

"Please don't do that," he requested politely. "In case you haven't noticed, we're thirty thousand feet in the air."

She looked around. An airplane, of course. A private jet, with furniture instead of airline seats. A small sofa, comfortable chairs, a wet bar. Reading lamps, a fold-down desk. Fax machine, telephones, television and VCR. A *corporate* jet.

The St. Clare Corporation.

She demanded hoarsely, "Where are you taking me? Why are you doing this?"

"All in good time, my dear." Firmly he guided her back to the sofa and made her sit down.

In another moment, he returned with two aspirin in a paper cup and a cut-glass goblet filled with ice water. She regarded them suspiciously.

"They're perfectly safe," he assured her impatiently. "If I'd wanted to poison you, I would have done it by now."

She hesitated another moment, more out of principle than any real doubt, then took the aspirin and swallowed them with water.

Noel lounged across from her in a plush club chair, picking up a champagne flute he had left on the table. "Have some?" he offered, indicating the glass. "It's Dom Perignon."

She stared at him stonily.

He sipped the champagne. "Perhaps later," he murmured, but his eyes were alert, watching her.

"It's true, isn't it?" he said in a moment, and his voice held a subdued note of amazement and curiosity. "You've showered, but I can smell him on you. You've been with him." His eyes narrowed. "How is that possible?"

A dull heat started at the tips of Aggie's toes and crept over her entire body, stealing out of her collar, flaming in her face. Her fists tightened in her lap and she said not a word.

Noticing her embarrassment, Noel chuckled. Aggie

was dismayed to note that he had a truly nice laugh. When he smiled, he looked, well, human.

"Thank God we're not that shy," he said. He regarded her frankly as he sipped his champagne. "One thing you'll learn quickly if you're around our kind very much, there aren't many secrets. All in all, a much healthier way to live, I think, than what you humans have devised with all your silly pruderies and constraints. There are no sex crimes among our people, did you know that?"

And when she determinedly said nothing, he excused her rudeness with a graceful lift of his shoulders and another sip of champagne. His gaze became speculative, tinged with an interest that was undeniably prurient. "Tell me, did he...that is to say, how did you...?" And then he held up a hand with a wince of something that very closely resembled distaste. "No, wait, don't tell me. I'm quite sure that's something I really don't want to know." He took a quick sip of champagne, as though to clear his palate.

Aggie said quietly, "You are contemptible."

He smiled thoughtfully, unoffended. "Michael mated with a human," he mused out loud. "An interesting development indeed. And all the better for me, I should think."

He fell silent, drumming his slender fingers lightly upon the arm of the chair, sipping his champagne, apparently ruminating on this.

When Aggie couldn't stand it any longer, she burst out, "What have you done with Michael? Did you kill him in his sleep?"

The look of shock and disgust on his face could not have been feigned. "Good God, woman, of course not! What do you think I am?"

"I *know* what you are," Aggie reminded him, clenching her fists even tighter in her lap to try to keep her voice from shaking. She wasn't entirely successful. "You murdered that man in the garage. You…" Her voice caught. She couldn't help it. "You tore his throat out."

Noel relaxed back in his chair. The wry twist to his lips was not unkind. "And of course no human has ever killed another one."

He gestured briefly with his champagne glass, sobering. "Gavin had to die. He had gone bad. Of course, it was my fault that he followed me that night. I should have been more careful. But he attacked in human form, with a *knife*. That's…" He frowned a little, as though looking for the words that would explain so complex an issue to her. "Well, it's simply unacceptable. It's against a cardinal moral law. And it's stupid.

"When I saw he had lost control," he went on, "I had a choice to make. I chose to destroy him before he killed Michael. Perhaps that was a mistake." He took a sip of his champagne, and a flicker of uncertainty, perhaps even anxiety, crossed those cool green eyes. "If so, I shall pay for it."

Then he smiled and indicated the champagne glass to her. "Are you sure you won't have some? We'll dine in an hour or so, but I believe there's some beluga in the fridge if you're hungry in the meantime."

Again she made no reply. She couldn't have spoken through her astonishment, even if she had wanted to. Murder. Champagne. Moral laws. Insanity. Caviar?

He shrugged and finished off his glass. "Suit yourself. But if you don't mind, I believe I'll have a short nap before lunch. I was up most of the night in that ghastly rain, it'll be a wonder if I don't catch my death.''

He set the empty glass on the table and smiled, stretching out his legs onto a low plush hassock. ''I believe we've established that any attempt at escape on your part would be self-defeating, haven't we?''

''You won't get away with this,'' Aggie said tightly. ''Michael will come for me.''

Noel looked surprised. ''Good heavens, I hope so.'' He settled more comfortably in the chair and folded his hands across his spare middle. ''After all this trouble, I do most certainly hope so.''

He closed his eyes and, incredibly, went to sleep.

CHAPTER FIFTEEN

The bed in which Aggie awoke was a giant four-poster hung with tapestry drapes. The mattress felt like a cloud, the pillows that surrounded her were soft enough to drown in. She was wearing a nightgown of softest brushed cotton, and she was so warm and cozy, she didn't want to move.

The room was enormous. It had a high frescoed ceiling and mullioned windows hung with the same sort of heavy tapestry that decorated the bed. A fire crackled gaily in the marble fireplace and gave off the faint, comforting scent of hickory. The walls were hung with pale blue silk-moire and decorated with paintings and mirrors in gilt frames. There was an Oriental carpet on the floor and beneath it gleaming wooden planks. A sitting area was drawn up before one window featuring yellow silk Queen Anne chairs and a silver tea service. Aggie wondered if she was still dreaming.

She pushed to her elbows, struggling to sit up amidst the ocean of eiderdown comforters and fluffy pillows. On the plane, she recalled, Noel had served rare roast beef and potatoes with a rich red wine. Aggie had been unable to eat, but she'd drunk a great deal of the wine, simply to keep from shaking uncontrollably. She didn't remember much of anything after that. But her headache was gone.

At her movement, a figure turned from the window—no, two figures. One was a tall slender woman with waist-length silver hair. The other was a small brown wolf. Instinctively, Aggie pressed back against the headboard.

The wolf stopped politely a few feet from her and sat on the carpet, watching her with interest. The woman smiled. "Well, there you are, and no worse for wear, I trust. You've been asleep for almost twenty hours, we were beginning to worry."

Aggie passed a hand over her face, clearing her throat. She tried not to stare at the wolf. "He drugged the wine."

A trace of regret softened the woman's face as she nodded. "Well, yes. He thought it was best to take no chances when you transferred to the helicopter in Fairbanks. It was for your own safety."

"Noel seems to have a pretty free hand with drugs," Aggie observed humorlessly. And then she couldn't help it; she shot a nervous look at the wolf. The wolf cocked its head at her curiously. Aggie looked quickly away.

The woman agreed pleasantly. "Well, yes, I suppose he does. But then he is a chemist."

She had a lovely face, though as she drew closer, Aggie realized she was older than her youthful figure had at first indicated. The long hair might once have been blond, and the lines around her eyes and mouth, though fine, suggested a woman well into her seventies. Her eyes were sapphire blue.

Aggie sat up straighter, trying to look imposing. It was difficult to do in a bed that made her feel like a china doll adrift in a sea of pillows, and with a wolf watching her every move. "Where am I?" she demanded, but in fact it sounded more like a timid request.

"You are at Castle St. Clare, Alaska," the woman replied with a smile. "I am Clarice St. Clare, Michael's mother. This—" she gestured to the wolf "—is Adrienne." She looked as though she might clarify the relationship further, then thought better of it. "I hope you don't mind her being here, but she's young and curious. She's not to get underfoot, however," she added sternly as the wolf stood up and started to approach the bed. The wolf sat again, panting in what looked for all the world like a sheepish grin.

Aggie dragged her gaze away from the wolf and back to the woman. Michael's mother. Alaska. Castle...

She said weakly, "I don't understand."

The other woman's expression grew sympathetic. "Of course you don't. This is a dreadful business, all of it, and you must have a hundred questions. But first, you've had a long trip and you'll want to take care of personal comforts. The bath is just there..." She indicated a silk-paneled door on the opposite wall. "And I've taken the liberty of having some clothes brought up for you. September in Alaska is a little cooler than you're used to, although it's such a fine day today, I thought you might like to walk with me in the garden later. We'll have a good long talk. Meanwhile, I'll have a tray sent up for you. I'm sure you're starving."

With a final smile, she beckoned to the young wolf. "Come along, Adrienne."

With every appearance of reluctance, the wolf got to its feet and followed the woman to the door. Clarice said, "Just pick up the phone on the desk when you're ready, and someone will come to escort you out."

Aggie swallowed hard. "Am I a prisoner then?"

The woman's laugh was as musical as bells. "Of

course not! You're free to come and go as you please. But this place is so enormous, you could easily become lost for days if you took a wrong turn, and I don't want to waste a moment of our time together.''

She opened the door, then looked back. ''Noel, by the way, sends his apologies for any discomfort he may have caused you. He was raised to treat females with respect—even human ones—though I sometimes think he only remembers his upbringing when it suits him.'' A shadow of purely maternal disapproval briefly tightened the lines around her mouth, and was gone. She added gently, ''Please believe me when I say that from this moment on, we will all do everything in our power to make your stay with us as pleasant as possible.''

It was impossible to doubt a woman whose smile was so sincere, whose eyes were so much like her son's. Michael's mother. Aggie latched on to that and held on to the hope. If Michael's mother was here, then everything would be all right. She would know if Michael was hurt, she would care. Aggie wasn't entirely alone anymore.

The bathroom was like something out of a designer magazine. It contained a pink marble Roman tub and a separate, teak-lined shower and sauna room. A sunlamp flooded the room with radiant light and fluffy bath sheets were kept warm on heated racks. Apothecary jars on staggered glass shelves contained lotions, bath beads and powders in a variety of exotic scents. Aggie thought she knew the meaning of luxury, but this was beyond anything she had ever even imagined.

She showered, and dressed in silk underwear, soft cotton jeans and a big cable-knit sweater that had been left for her. When she returned to her room, a breakfast feast had been set before the fire. It was as though the chef, uncertain what she liked, had decided to send up one of everything, and she laughed out loud as she lifted cover after cover. Eggs Benedict, mushroom omelet, ham, steak and bacon, at least a dozen different kinds of pastries, lox and bagels, a selection of cheeses, fresh fruit, clotted cream. Coffee, tea and three different juices.

She found she was hungrier than she thought, and managed to do justice to the eggs Benedict and several of the pastries, marveling that there were actually people in the world who lived like this…and Michael was one of them. It was when she thought of Michael that her chest clenched in anxiety and longing. Where was he? He must have discovered by now what had happened and would be out of his mind with worry. Did he know where she had been taken? What if he couldn't find her?

Surely he would listen to the message on the answering machine, see the fax and reach the same conclusion she had. Even if he couldn't remember, he would find her.

What if they wouldn't *let* him find her? What if…

She paced to the window and looked out anxiously, but all she could see were evergreens and mountains. Her windows faced a wilderness. When she couldn't stand it anymore, she picked up the French-style telephone on the escritoire and a cheerful female voice informed her that Madame St. Clare was waiting for her in the south garden. If she would go to her door, she would find a young man ready to escort her down. The temperature outside was forty-six degrees. She should please dress warmly.

When she asked, Aggie was informed after a surprised pause that no, it would not be possible for her to place an outside call.

With no other choices, Aggie opened her door and indeed found a sandy-haired young man waiting in the corridor. Though he didn't say much, he did manage to act more like an escort than a guard as he led her through a maze of high-ceilinged stone corridors, into an elevator, across a magnificent gallery filled with paintings which, if they weren't original masterpieces, were incredibly good copies.

They passed others in the halls, some people, some wolves; wolves and people all watched her with interest. Occasionally, a man or a woman would favor her with a nod of acknowledgment or a faint smile. Down one branching corridor she heard the sounds of ringing telephones and clacking printers, from another the strains of an opera. Once, a group of laughing children cut across their path and received a sharp reprimand from Aggie's escort. Like children everywhere, they slowed down until they were out of sight then burst into high-spirited leaps and shrieks again.

Aggie was grateful she had not been left to attempt to find her way downstairs on her own, particularly when she realized, from the many unexplored stairways and corridors they passed, that she had not even reached the main part of the house. Her escort took her down a wide, palazzo-like flight of stairs and through an arboretum filled with breathtaking tropical plants and trees and the scent of orchids. Finally, he pushed open a set of enormous doors inset with stained glass, and they stepped out onto a flagstone path lined with tall heather. Her escort pointed out a kitchen garden, now stripped of all but the hardiest greens, a grape arbor, barren this time of year, and finally the south garden. Clarice St. Clare, in a form-fitting, ankle-length woolen dress and portrait hat tied with a scarf, looked every bit the lady of the manor as she wandered among the rosebushes with a basket over one arm. A little girl with curly brown hair accompanied her, carrying a basket of pruning tools. Several wolves of varied sizes wandered around or lounged in the sun, and it wasn't just her imagination that told Aggie they all took particular note of her when she passed.

Clarice St. Clare lifted her hand to Aggie when she saw her and Aggie's escort bowed, first to the older woman, then to her, before he took his leave. Aggie joined her near a bush that, incredibly, still held a few deep red blossoms. The little girl smiled shyly at Aggie. Aggie smiled back.

"Roses in Alaska this time of year," she marveled as Clarice clipped a blossom and let it fall into her basket. "They're beautiful."

Clarice smiled in gratification. "We've worked very hard to develop the strain. It's been a multigenerational project. Of course, soon they'll have to be dug up for the winter—they're only hardy to minus ten— but I'm so pleased to get these last few lovely blooms."

She handed her flower basket to the little girl. "There now, Adrienne, take these in to Aunt Win and ask her to find a vase for you. We shall use these on the dinner table tonight."

"Yes, *Grand-maman*."

The little girl skipped off and Aggie stared after her.

"She's my youngest granddaughter." Clarice's expression was indulgent as she watched the little girl go. "I spoil her, but she's only here for a short time.

The family just flew in from Paris last night. As a matter of fact, we have quite a full house at the moment, because of..." And her expression altered slightly as she glanced at Aggie. "Well, because of the trouble."

Aggie said tensely, "I don't understand any of this. Maybe you don't want me to, maybe *I* don't want to. All I care about is Michael. If you know anything at all—"

Clarice slipped her hand through Aggie's arm, her expression filled with sympathy and a reflection of Aggie's own concern. She said, "My dear, I promise you, the moment I know something, you will. For now, all we can do is wait."

How long? Aggie wanted to scream. And in the meantime, what was happening to the man she loved?

But Clarice said, "Come, walk with me a bit. Let me see if I can make some of this easier to understand."

They started down the path. A large black wolf jumped down from a sunny bench to follow them. Another appeared from the opposite side of the garden and fell into step beside him. Aggie realized they were body-guards. The St. Clare version of the Secret Service. She felt a hysterical urge to laugh.

"Michael is my youngest, you know," Clarice went on serenely. "Traditionally, the youngest inherits—unlike your monarchies, which I believe have always been passed down through the eldest. We came to Alaska centuries ago, from France, from Russia, from countries whose names now are no longer in existence. The St. Clares have been the ruling family now for almost four hundred years, much like your Windsors of England." And she turned a curious, pleasant look on Aggie. "I wonder, my dear, do you know the queen?"

Mutely, Aggie shook her head.

"Such a lovely woman. I had hoped we might dine again before..." And she sighed and resumed her walk. "At any rate, Michael, as brilliant as he is, as well suited as he has been bred to be for command, has always been rebellious. A certain amount of adventuresome spirit is of course to be applauded, but with Michael...his father would never admit it, but I always suspected it was something more. And now I have been proven right, in this most horrible way.

"It was time for him to assume the mantle of command," she explained simply. "For years, he has steadfastly refused to talk about the eventuality, even though his natural leadership abilities continued to take him higher and higher in the company. You must understand that positions within the corporation are not granted, no matter who you are. Everyone earns his own way."

For the first time, Aggie felt compelled to interrupt. "I don't understand about the company. Is everyone in the entire corporation—the entire, multibillion dollar, international corporation—like, well, like you?"

She smiled. "We do not engage in discriminatory hiring practices, if that's what you mean. We do have some humans working for us in low-level positions but, frankly, they invariably lack the necessary skills to rise within the company."

When Aggie just stared at her, she explained, "The same advanced evolution that enabled us to survive for centuries in the forest—indeed, to endure the unwarranted persecution inflicted upon us for so many years by those of *your* kind, my dear—are the very same skills that, today, have made us kings of a very different kind of jungle.''

Aggie still looked blank, and Clarice smiled. ''If your sense of hearing were five hundred times sharper than that of any human's in the world, might not you learn certain things from time to time that would give you a distinct advantage over your competitors? And if your sense of smell were more acute than that of any creature on the planet, it does follow that you might create some of the most exquisite perfumes ever devised. And that, of course, is only the beginning. In the faraway past, the survival of the pack depended upon the skills of our hunters. Now it depends upon our business and financial acumen. Family loyalty is very strong among our kind, and for that reason, we are all involved in the company in one way or another.''

''Amazing,'' Aggie murmured. ''Simply amazing.'' Then, ''How many of you are there?''

She fluttered a graceful hand. ''Oh, I'd have to get out the pack tree for that. Hundreds and hundreds.''

''All over the world?''

''Well, not *all* over. We have offices in Paris, Montreal, New York, Moscow, Tokyo, Hong Kong, London, Amsterdam…'' And she laughed lightly. ''Well, almost all over, I suppose.''

''And you're all…?'' Aggie didn't know the word.

She smiled. ''One of your kind coined the word *werewolf* many centuries ago. We don't find the term offensive. The name we call ourselves would be unpronounceable to your tongue, I'm afraid.''

''And you live in apartment buildings and take taxicabs and are listed on the New York stock exchange and everything? You make sales calls and play golf and go to the theater just like…just like…''

Clarice seemed amused. ''My dear, we own most of the theaters in New York and London. We're very interested in the arts.''

Aggie felt a chill. She stopped walking. ''Wait a minute.'' Her voice was a little hoarse. ''Why are you telling me this?''

Clarice lifted an eyebrow. ''I thought you wanted to know.''

''But I'm a writer.''

Clarice looked interested. ''Are you now? How lovely for you. My grandson—Noel's brother's boy, actually—is a writer. He writes novels about ghosts and witches and people from outer space. I think it's all nonsense, of course, though I would never tell him so. And apparently he does quite well for himself. He was on the *Times* bestseller list for forty-one weeks last year.''

It took more willpower than Aggie had ever known she possessed not to ask who the grandson was. But did she really want to know?

Focus, focus…

She cleared her throat. ''What I mean is, aren't you afraid I'll repeat what you've told me? That I'll write about it? Or…'' And she caught her breath in anticipation of the reply. ''Don't you intend to ever let me leave here?''

Clarice laughed again and squeezed her arm, drawing her back into place on their walk. ''My dear, what do we care what you write? You'll hardly be the first.''

It was true, Aggie realized with a sinking sense of relief that was oddly mingled with disappointment. Who would believe her if she told?

She said, "Tell me about Noel."

"He is our oldest daughter's son, very bright, very capable. Because of the closeness in their ages, he and Michael have always been somewhat competitive. Not in an unfriendly way, of course, but in sports, in school, even to some extent within the company, he and Michael have always run neck and neck." She looked unhappy. "In many ways, I love Noel as my own. I don't think he ever intended things to turn out as they have done with Michael."

They rounded a corner and suddenly, spread before Aggie in all its magnificence, was a crystal-blue glacier lake. Towering evergreens and snowcapped mountains were reflected on its surface, couples strolled arm in arm along the shore, children tossed stones into the water, wolves rolled and tumbled together on the browning carpet of grass that surrounded it.

Aggie dropped the older woman's arm and stood still, her eyes suddenly filling with tears of joy, of remembrance. She whispered, "I know this place!"

She left Clarice, and ran toward the water, dropping down beside an oddly shaped projection of granite, caressing it, pressing her face to its sun-warmed surface. Michael was everywhere. This was his home. *She* was home.

Clarice followed her quickly, her face marked with concern. Aggie looked up at her, laughing and crying as she said, "He used to play here. This is the jumping rock. They would climb on it as children and jump into the water. And here…"

She leaped to her feet, rushing down a path between the pines, turning a corner, passing a collection of stone benches and picnic tables, until she stopped before a larger than life-size statue of a wolf.

"They used to take turns riding the wolf," she said, breathless with happiness. "Once, he fell off and scraped his knee. He still has the scar."

She whirled to Clarice, pressing her hands to her face, glowing with happiness. Michael. This was his, all of it, his. And being here meant she was near him.

Clarice took a careful step toward her. Her expression was watchful. "Michael told you?"

Aggie's face grew even hotter. No woman, looking into her eyes, could deny the truth that glowed there. She said, "Not exactly."

Clarice's fingers went to her lips, then touched her throat. She avoided Aggie's eyes. She said after a moment, and with obvious difficulty, "Oh...my. Noel told us, but I couldn't..." She looked quickly back at Aggie, her expression uncertain, almost pleading. "Michael forms very strong attachments, even with humans. That isn't unusual, there's even a certain kind of honor to it. But this...I..." She spread her hands in a gesture of helplessness. "I really don't know what to say."

Aggie knew she had upset the other woman, but she refused to feel guilty for it. Michael had been with her, in these last few brief moments of recognition, and the reality of what they had shared, of what they were to each other, gave her the strength to face anything.

She lifted her chin, and she said, "I love your son, Madame St. Clare. With all my heart and soul and everything I ever hope to be, I love him. I'm sorry if this upsets you."

Clarice took a step toward her, her face immediately

softening into sympathy and concern. "Oh, my dear, no." She cupped Aggie's cheek tenderly. "It's I who am sorry—for you."

She slipped an arm around Aggie's shoulders and led her to a bench they had passed. "Come, sit with me. Tell me everything, from the beginning."

As best she could, stumbling over the parts she still did not understand, Aggie told Michael's mother what had happened to her son in the time since she had last seen him. Clarice seemed to age with every word Aggie spoke.

"So," Clarice said at last, staring out into the distance. "It's true what Noel said. His mind is gone."

"Not his mind," Aggie corrected quickly. "His memory. And even it had mostly returned by the time I—when Noel kidnapped me," she said, and didn't try to keep the bitterness out of her voice.

Clarice looked at her urgently. "But he did experience the change, you're sure of it?"

Aggie nodded. "And then he, well, I think he tried to kill himself, when he went through the glass door. He was so confused, he didn't understand, and he hated what was happening to him. But after we made love, I think he *did* understand. He wasn't ashamed anymore."

Tears glittered in Clarice's eyes. "My poor child. How he must have suffered. I never knew. I never knew how tormented he must have been inside."

"I think," Aggie said carefully, "all he ever wanted was to live his own life. To discover for himself who he wanted to be. And when he forgot his past, he had a chance to do that. He was happy with me," she said simply. "Even with all that he had troubling him, he was happy."

Clarice took both of Aggie's hands in hers and squeezed them tightly. "And for that, my dear, dear child, you have my undying gratitude."

Then she sighed and looked away. "But this creates more problems than you can know."

"I—I do know," Aggie stammered, and was suddenly shy. "Madame St. Clare, please tell me if this is inappropriate, but I don't know who else to ask. Is it—is it always like that, the connection, I mean, the visions, when you make love?"

The other woman's kind smile almost, but not completely, eased Aggie's embarrassment. "For us it is," she answered gently. "For you, for humans, well, frankly, I don't believe there's anyone who could tell you. It's not something that's commonly done, you must understand, this…cross-species consorting. And I must be honest, it's certainly not a practice we would condone. Fortunately it's not a problem we've ever had to regulate because, to be honest, our kind doesn't generally find your kind, well, attractive."

Aggie hid a smile. She was quite certain she had been insulted, but it didn't matter. The only thing that mattered was that *one* of their kind found her attractive.

She said, "Michael thought—and forgive me again if I'm being indelicate—but at first we were afraid he couldn't…that is to say, he didn't think it was possible for him to make love in human form."

The other woman looked thoughtful for a moment. "Again, that's not a question that's very often asked. It's possible, I suppose…but why? I mean, what would be the point? It's quite against nature, don't you think?"

Then she looked at Aggie, seemed to realize what

she had said and blushed prettily. Her expression was wry. "Perhaps you're right. It is an indelicate subject, and certainly not one upon which I am an authority."

And then she sobered. Once again she took Aggie's hands in hers. "Aggie, you are a charming human and I can see why my son was enchanted with you. You will have a friend among us for as long as you live for what you have done for him. But surely you realize that this...liaison...is quite impossible. You are not his *kind*. Michael's duty is to breed an heir, and you must realize that, all other considerations aside, any match between you would be a sterile one. You could never produce progeny."

Aggie stared at her. She had not thought of that. No children. A sterile match. *Not his kind...*

Clarice's expression softened in understanding. "Oh, you poor dear. I do understand. I believe that you love my son. I believe that he loves you. But what will happen when his memory returns completely? You know so little about us. Will you still love him so when you *really* understand what it is to be one of us? My dear, please. I know it hurts. But you must prepare yourself. This insanity must end."

Aggie couldn't answer. She wanted to, but no words would come. And in the end, she was saved the effort of a reply when a young man came quickly up the path toward them. Clarice rose to meet him. He bent to whisper something in her ear.

Clarice turned, her face pale but composed. "It's Michael," she said. "He is coming."

With a cry, Aggie leaped to her feet. She started to rush past Clarice, but the older woman caught her arm. There was immense sorrow in her eyes.

"Now you are about to learn more of us than you

want to know," she said quietly. "Noel didn't know about your connection with Michael when he took you. For a friend, Michael would fight. But for a lover, he will kill."

CHAPTER SIXTEEN

Chaos erupted long before Aggie and Clarice reached the house. The news spread like wildfire. Wolves and wolves in human form streamed in from the meadows and forests, rushed through the corridors. The atmosphere was tense and charged with expectation, and the air was so thick with excitement that it actually tasted electric to Aggie's tongue.

As they reached the back door, Clarice suddenly turned and thrust Aggie into the arms of two guards. They may or may not have been the wolves who had been following them; now they were in human form.

"Take her to him," Clarice said. "Quickly." She seemed tense and excited, and there was a glitter to her eyes that could have been tears. But she took a moment to pat Aggie's arm and assure her, "You'll be all right, don't be afraid. Do as you're told."

The older woman moved quickly away.

Aggie went with the guards into the house and down several flights of steps, into a series of stone tunnels. At times, she had to run to keep up, for the excitement that had permeated the entire compound had not left them untouched. Their footsteps clattered in the tunnels and Aggie's gasping breaths echoed. The atmosphere would have unnerved even the most sanguine of visitors had they been alone in the tunnels, but even there, hurrying footsteps padded and wolf claws clacked.

Finally, they reached a wooden door built into the

stone wall, and Aggie was pushed inside. The doors closed and she heard a bolt turn on the other side.

The stone chamber was small, roughly hewn out of what appeared to be a natural rock surface. It was lit only by candlelight, which surprised Aggie because even the tunnels had been illuminated by fluorescent tubes. Rock ledges projected from the walls and there was the sound of water dripping in close by. It looked and smelled ancient.

A figure materialized from the shadowy corner and came toward her. Aggie gave a joyful cry and took a running step to meet him, then stopped. It wasn't Michael. It was Noel.

"Thank God," he said tensely. He unfastened onyx cuff links and stuffed them into his pants pockets, then started to unbutton his shirt. "I was afraid they wouldn't find you in time."

Aggie stared at him. Something cold and clammy crept over her as she began to understand. "Where is Michael?" she demanded hoarsely.

He pulled his shirt out of his waistband and off his shoulders, shaking out the wrinkles before draping it over a shelf. "At last report, about five hundred meters away." His smile was tight and bitter as he unfastened his belt and pulled it free. "And you were afraid he wouldn't find you."

"I knew he would find me," she said, shaking with suppressed anger and fear and sudden, absolute understanding. "And so did you."

He unbuttoned his trousers. "At last, somebody is giving me credit. I counted on an emotional jolt to bring Michael back to himself. I had to make him mad enough, and frightened enough, to bring out the old instincts. And it worked." His expression was grim. "Maybe too well."

He lowered his zipper and stepped out of his pants. Aggie backed up against the door.

"What are you doing?" It was not much above a gasp.

"What does it look like?" He scowled impatiently as he stripped off his socks. "For God's sake, I don't have time for your stupid human modesty now. Turn your head if you're offended. Damn, it's cold in here."

Aggie whirled and gripped the door handle, struggling with it frantically. Noel was upon her in an instant, dragging her back. She turned on him, swinging her fists, clawing at him. "Let me go!" she screamed.

His hand clamped down hard over her mouth. "Stop that infernal shrieking! Are you mad?"

She tried to bite his hand but couldn't, tried to wrench away but he was incredibly strong. He was breathing hard as he subdued her struggles, but more from outrage, she thought, than exertion.

"What's the matter with you?" he demanded. "What do you think I'm going to do—rape you?" And he looked disdainful. "Good Lord, I wouldn't know how to begin. Now stop this. Act like a woman. Michael will be here any minute, do you want him to see you like this?"

He gave her a little shake, then released her abruptly. She fell back against the door as he strode across the room, naked, and picked up a woolen cloak.

"You bastard!" she gasped, still shaking. She wanted to launch herself at him, kicking and clawing, but knew her knees would not support her halfway across the room. She pressed her hands against the wooden door to keep herself upright. "You set him up! You used me as bait to draw him here and now you're going to attack him, to kill him—"

Noel swung the cloak around his shoulders and turned on her, eyes blazing. "Do you think I wanted this?" he cried. "Do you think if in my wildest imaginings... There hasn't been a ritual like this in four hundred years! I counted on Grand-père to intervene, to issue an edict. No one expected *this!*"

He pushed an agitated hand through his blond hair. "I've never beaten Michael in a contest in my life. Do you really think I'd be fool enough to challenge him to one that *meant* my life? You're worried about him? Look at me! I'm the one you should be sorry for!"

She did look at him, and she saw a man who was white-faced with fear, but grim with determination. Under other circumstances, she might have seen the nobility in that, but at that moment she could not see beyond her own terror.

Noel said, more calmly, "Look, I'm sorry you've been dragged into this. But I didn't choose you, Michael did. When you became involved with Michael, you took on all of us, and the three thousand years of history that makes us what we are. Just remember, all of our world will be watching you today. If you care for Michael, don't shame him." And he took a breath. "Or me."

Suddenly, a look came over his face that made the small hairs on the back of Aggie's neck prickle. His eyes narrowed and his pupils went oval; he cocked his head in a posture of intense listening. He looked back at her. "It's time," he said.

He gripped her arm hard as he took a key from the

shelf by the door and unlocked it. She could hear the quickness of his breath, and the strength of his fingers hurt her.

"You don't have to do anything." He opened the door and dragged her through, moving quickly down the stone corridor. "Just for God's sake, try to control yourself. No more hysterics."

He stopped for a moment and looked at her seriously. "When it starts, go to *Grand-mère*. Don't try to intervene. We have to do this, do you understand? There's nothing you can do to stop it." And he repeated under his breath, mostly to himself, "We have to do this."

They emerged into a huge stone amphitheater the like of which had not been seen since the days of Rome. The walls were lined from top to bottom with stone benches; the benches were filled with shouting, roaring, howling, snapping men, women, children and wolves. Upon a dais behind Aggie and Noel were two enormous stone thrones. On one sat Clarice, draped in a magnificent white fur cape and wearing a silver diadem atop her head. Her demeanor was regal, her face tightly drawn. Next to her was the man Aggie immediately recognized as Sebastian St. Clare, Michael's father. His cloak was a patchwork of many different kinds and colors of fur, and in his hand he held an imposing, intricate carved wooden scepter. He showed no more emotion than his wife at the spectacle unfolding before them.

The cacophony assaulted Aggie's senses, inciting within her every atavistic instinct known to man. She was repulsed, she was horrified, she was excited, she was compelled. She wanted to run away; she couldn't have made herself run away. Fights broke out in the stands. Children shrieked. It was a circus.

No it was a gladiator fight.

And then she saw him. A roar went up among the crowd and then died into absolute silence as Michael, in full magnificent wolf form, entered the stadium.

She knew him immediately, and would have known him anywhere. The strength of form and posture, the lustrous coat with its distinctive V-shaped white streak, the sapphire blue eyes. Aggie's heart caught in her chest and only Noel's restraining grip on her arm kept her from running to him. Michael advanced, his tail down, his shoulders low, his lips drawn back in a snarl. And then he saw her. But did he recognize her?

Noel never took his eyes off Michael. With one hand, he reached up and unfastened his cloak. With the other, he pushed Aggie behind him. Michael gave a low, rolling growl that reverberated deep in the core of Aggie's soul. He launched himself at Noel. Noel sprang to meet him.

It was an incredible thing to watch. As Noel leaped, he transformed, shedding his human skin in a shimmering explosion of light and energy. The air was acrid with the speed and power of it. They met in midair, light wolf and dark wolf, in a shattering clash of teeth and muscle that sounded like thunder in the stillness of the stadium.

It *was* thunder, the thunderous roar of the crowd as the two wolves threw each other to the ground. Fur flew and blood splattered; the roars and growls of the combatants echoed even above the sounds of the spectators, they seemed to shake the very foundations of the earth.

Aggie screamed and rushed forward, and then she

felt a restraining arm around her shoulders. Clarice held her, urging her gently backward. Aggie wanted to fling her off, she wanted to scream at her, *They're killing each other, don't you see that?* But then she remembered Noel's words. The whole of their world was watching. *Don't shame him.*

And in Clarice's eyes, she saw the question. Was she ready to be one of them? Could she love Michael for all that he was?

She let herself be led back to the dais, where she could do nothing but watch as the man she loved destroyed himself for her sake.

Sebastian St. Clare did not even glance at Aggie as she took her place between the two thrones. All of his attention was focused on the battle, as though he was willing strength to the contestants. Clarice took her seat again, straight-backed and composed. Aggie gripped the stone arm of the throne until her nails cracked, one by one, tears streaming down her cheeks as she watched the horror unfold before her.

Michael, who had wanted only to live a human life. He asked nothing but peace, and order and civility, now he was forced to become the thing he hated most. To lose the battle would mean his life. But if he won it…if he killed Noel and gained control of a throne he didn't want…he would have won nothing. Such a victory would destroy him.

Aggie closed her eyes and she prayed, foolishly and futilely, to turn back time, to erase all the events of the past month that had led to this moment. If it meant she would never have met him, never have known him at all, it would be worth it to spare him this.

The dust was thick and it was hard to see. The combatants were sometimes close, sometimes far away.

The sounds of savagery were soul-chilling. They broke apart briefly and circled each other. The pale fur around Noel's neck was soaked with blood and he was limping. There was a gash on Michael's flank and his left ear dripped blood. Both were exhausted. Aggie felt, rather than heard, Clarice's soft catch of breath, and the fierce stiffening of her body was a reflection of Aggie's own tension. They both knew the battle could not go on much longer. The next attack would be the last.

Aggie saw the contraction of Michael's muscles, the narrowing of his eyes, an instant before it happened. In a heart-stopping display of the strength, speed and power that proved him worthy of his legacy, Michael launched the attack. A roar went up from the crowd and his assault was decisive. Before another breath could be drawn, Noel was on the ground and Michael's teeth closed on his throat.

''*Michael!*'' Aggie screamed.

He could not possibly have heard her over the thunder of the bloodthirsty crowd, but suddenly his eyes met hers, and it was Michael. Beneath the wildness, beneath the savagery of an ancestral past long denied, there was Michael. There was the man who could reason, the man who could remember, the man who could love. And he knew, as clearly as she did, what his choices were. His eyes filled with sorrow.

For the first time since she'd returned to the dais, Clarice moved, her nails digging sharply into Aggie's arm. Aggie pressed her fingers to her lips, holding back sobs. *Michael, please...* Tears streamed down her face and filled her throat, but she dared not make a sound.

Michael looked at Noel, and he looked at Aggie. Slowly, he relaxed his grip.

In an instant, their positions were reversed. Noel pinned Michael to the ground, his sides heaving, his teeth bared. And then, in the most beautiful act of purest nobility Aggie had ever seen, Michael arched his neck, baring his throat to his enemy.

Stillness gripped the crowd. Not a breeze stirred through the vast amphitheater, not even the sound of a breath disturbed the silence. Dust hung thick and sharp in the air, and more than a life hung in the balance as Noel hesitated, looking into Michael's eyes.

Then Noel stepped away, turned toward the dais, and sat down.

Sebastian St. Clare got to his feet. Aggie saw a tear tremble on the corner of the old man's eye, but there was not another flicker of emotion on his face. He lifted his arms. The two combatants got to their feet and shook themselves. The transformation swirled with dark colors as they returned to their human forms.

The two men knelt before the dais, heads bowed, hair tangled, their bodies slick with sweat and matted with dust, bleeding from their various wounds. With a muffled cry, Aggie lurched toward Michael, but the bite of Clarice's nails on her arm stopped her.

Slowly, Sebastian descended the steps. The silence was as tense as a held breath. He paused as he passed his son, and looked down at him. Aggie's heart caught. Then Sebastian moved on, and stood before Noel.

He removed his many-furred cloak and draped it over Noel's shoulders. Sebastian St. Clare took Noel's hand and raised him to his feet. The crowd leaped up, roaring its approval of the new leader.

Only Aggie wept for Michael, who remained kneeling, his head bowed, his eyes lowered.

The enthusiasm from the stands died away into curious murmurs, and Aggie swiped at her blurry, swollen eyes, trying to focus on what was happening. Finally, Clarice's death grip relaxed on her arm.

Noel walked away and picked up his own discarded cloak. Shaking out the dust, he returned to Michael and draped it over his shoulders. Michael looked up at him. Noel extended his hand, and helped Michael to his feet.

Quietly, but very clearly, he said, "I only hope I can be half as good at it as you would have been."

Michael smiled, and the crowd roared again as the two men embraced.

Aggie did not see Michael for two days. After the battle, Michael and Noel were led away by men in dark clothes, whom Aggie later learned were surgeons. She learned through the grapevine that Michael required a few stitches but was mending nicely. Noel had not fared so well, with a dislocated shoulder and several broken ribs. It had taken tremendous courage for him to continue fighting under those circumstances, but not as much courage as it had taken for him to back away from the fight at the end, to follow Michael's lead and refuse to take the life of a friend. Aggie did not like being indebted to Noel, and she didn't want to like him. But she couldn't help admiring him.

Clarice had breakfast with her once but seemed distant and distracted. She told Aggie only that Michael would be sequestered with what she called the "council'' for several days, preparing for the change of command.

Aggie did not know if he asked after her, or thought about her. She didn't know if he wanted her here. She didn't know anything at all.

On a cool late afternoon, Aggie sat on the jumping rock, her legs encircled by her arms, her chin resting on her knees, looking out over the lake. She felt his approach, and then his shadow, and then the light touch of his hands as he draped a soft woolen shawl around her shoulders.

Hope spiraled and danced inside her as she turned to him. He looked beautiful. Wearing jeans and a dark blue fisherman's sweater, his hair swept back, the setting sun on his face...a face that was carefully expressionless, eyes that were controlled and remote.

He said, "I don't know if anyone has told you, but we have transportation available to take you back anytime you say."

The hope that had sprung to life shriveled and died and was consumed by a cold knot of pain deep in her chest. She turned away, focusing hard on the lake. It was a long time before she could speak. "Do you want me to leave?"

A heartbeat passed before he said, "I can't keep you."

She looked up at him, pain and helplessness tearing across her face. "You don't have to," she whispered.

Swiftly, he dropped beside her on the rock, drawing her into his arms, pressing her head into his chest. "Oh, Aggie, how can I ask you to stay? How can I ask anything of you? Now that you know...now that you've seen...how can I expect you to understand?"

Aggie pushed away from him, swiping an angry

hand across her wet eyes. "Damn you, Michael. How dare you say that to me? How dare you think I wouldn't understand? After all we've been through together, how dare you think you have to *ask?*"

Once again, he reached for her, closing his eyes as he drew her, unprotesting, back into his arms. "Aggie, Aggie," he said softly. "I love you so much."

"You told me," she said thickly against his chest, "that you mate for life. I believed you."

His arms tightened. "It's true. We do."

She lifted her face to him. "So do I."

He kissed the salt from her cheeks, closed her eyes with his lips, tasted her mouth, drew in her scent like the breath of life. He held her, fiercely and tightly for a long time.

Then, slowly, he drew away. His face was sober. "There are things we can't ignore, Aggie. Since my memory returned, and these last few days, being home again, learning to accept my nature...I don't want to fight it anymore. This is what I *am,* and it's not altogether good...but not altogether bad. I think, believe it or not, I learned most of that from you."

She smiled, closing her hand around his. "I know what you are. And believe it or not, I think I could even learn to like it...if you think you could learn to like being with a mere human."

He stroked her cheek, and his answer was in his eyes. But he grew sober again and dropped his hand.

"There is the other thing," he said quietly. "We can never have children. I know how much you want them."

Aggie dropped her eyes and was silent for a moment. "Yes," she said simply. "I've thought about it. What I wanted was a family." She looked up at him hesitantly. "There are a lot of children out there who could use a mother like me, and a father like you. We've so much to teach, both of us, so much to share—from your world and mine. We could adopt."

He looked at her in subdued wonder. "Would you do that for me?"

"Would you do it for me?"

He said, "Yes." And he drew her into his arms again. "Oh, Aggie, yes."

At length, they stood up and, arms around each other's waists, walked along the shore. For a long time, they didn't talk. Simply being near each other, feeling the closeness of each other, breathing in the taste of each other, was enough.

Then Michael said, "It's been so hard staying away from you these past days. I wanted to give you time to think, to decide if you could live with what you know about us now. And then there were my duties to the pack, and my family."

She said thoughtfully, "I understand about Noel being chosen the heir. But I don't understand what your position is now."

"I should have been exiled. By law, it was Noel's right to kill me. But when he acknowledged me before the pack, he made sure I would always have a home here—and perhaps more important, to them at least, a position in the company."

She looked up at him. "But you're no longer CEO?"

He chuckled. "Darling, I'll be lucky if I can get a position folding paper clips in this company now. Although I believe we are thinking of opening a plant in Siberia. Perhaps I could supervise the loading docks."

She looked at him in confusion and he squeezed her

waist, obviously undismayed by his limited prospects. "It's complicated, but even though I'm under Noel's protection, and still welcome in the pack, respect is something that is earned among us, in our business dealings as well as in our personal lives."

His voice grew thoughtful. "Unfortunately, I'm a little too arrogant to start at the bottom of the corporate ladder. And I'm tired of business. I liked building things, learning new skills." He flexed his hand before him. "I was thinking I would like to go into the construction trade."

Aggie laughed and pressed her head against his shoulder, adoring him.

"I'm very quick," he assured her. "I'm sure I can pick it up."

"I'm sure you can, too," she said. She felt radiant inside, glowing with happiness. "And maybe your first project could be enlarging my house. Making it big enough for two."

He stepped in front of her, smiling, and caught both of her hands. "That," he said, "sounds like an excellent idea."

He leaned forward and kissed her lips. Holding her hands straight down against her sides, he looked down at her, amusement glinting in his eyes. "I understand you had a...rather intimate talk with my mother."

Aggie nodded, a little embarrassed. "I had to ask."

He planted another teasing kiss on the edge of her mouth. "Did she answer all your questions?"

"Most of them."

He licked the lobe of her ear, the hollow of her neck, teased the inside of her mouth. Her hands tingled to caress him and he held them still. "I don't suppose anyone mentioned,'' he murmured against her neck, "that our appetites can sometimes be...voracious?"

Aggie pulled her hands away and thrust them into his hair, twisting firmly, pulling his face up to hers. "So can mine," she told him.

Their mouths met and passion flamed. Aggie melted into him, opening her mouth to receive him, drinking greedily of him. He pulled her close, pushing a knee between her legs. He unsnapped her jeans and slipped his hands inside, caressing her buttocks and her abdomen. Aggie tore her mouth away from his, gasping, "Inside. Let's go inside."

He smothered a chuckle in her neck. "Ah, yes. I almost forgot about your human modesty."

Aggie stepped away from him a fraction, her eyes sparking a promise. Slowly, she drew her nails up the front of his thighs. She saw his pupils widen with the dart of pleasure she created. "It's not my modesty I'm worried about," she told him throatily. "It's yours. Because the things I'm going to do to you I'm sure you don't want anyone to see."

With a low growl of surrender, he drew her to him. "I think you're right. Let's go inside. After all, we can't have *everyone* wanting to marry a human."

* * * * *

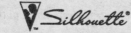